MURDER MAKES WAVES

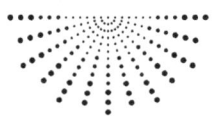

CARMEN RADTKE

Murder Makes Waves

A Jack and Frances mystery

Copyright © 2020 Carmen Radtke

The right of Carmen Radtke to be identified as the Author of the Work has been asserted by her in accordance with the Copyright, Designs and Patents Act 1988.

Published in 2020 by Adamantine Books, UK

Apart from any use permitted under UK copyright law, this publication may only be reproduced, stored, or transmitted, in any form, or by any means, with prior permission in writing of the publisher or, in the case of reprographic production, in accordance with the terms of licences issued by the Copyright Licensing Agency.

This book is a work of fiction. Any resemblance to real persons, living or dead, or real events is purely coincidental.

ISBN 978-1-9162410-4-6

One of my favourite characters in this book, Tinkerbell, was inspired by the most joyful little dog I've ever met. She spent her final months as a hospice dog, cared for and loved by screenwriter Tracee Beebe, who's opened her home and her heart to many elderly animals in similar circumstances.
This novel is dedicated to Tracee and everyone who fosters animals or supports their care. I can't imagine my life without a four-legged companion and the happiness they bring.

ALSO BY CARMEN RADTKE

Novels by Carmen Radtke

The Jack and Frances series:
A Matter of Love and Death
Murder at the Races
Murder Makes Waves

False Play at the Christmas Party (a Jack Sullivan quick read)

The Alyssa Chalmers series:
The Case of the Missing Bride
Glittering Death

Walking in the Shadow

Murder Makes Waves
By Carmen Radtke

CAST OF CHARACTERS

The passengers

- Jack Sullivan, nightclub owner, veteran and fiancé of
- Frances Palmer, amateur assistant of her godfather,
- "Salvatore the Magnificent" Bernardo, aka Uncle Sal, a vaudeville artist
- The Right Honourable Mildred Clifton, an admirer of Uncle Sal
- Tommy Clifton, her devoted nephew
- Tinkerbell, Mildred's corgi
- Doreen Halsall, widow and society lady
- Rosalie Halsall, her daughter
- Lawrence Vaughan, Rosalie's fiancé
- Mr Callaghan, a bad-tempered young man
- Mr Fitch, another young man
- Mr Brown, ditto
- Mr Sanders, ditto

- Major Forsythe, a self-important man who might not be what he seems

Assorted passengers

- The ship's crew
- Captain Grey, a troubled ship's master
- Mr Whalan, a resourceful First Officer
- Mr Mackie, a Second Officer in charge of the entertainers
- Evie, a singer and dancer with too many admirers
- Ada and Nancy, dancers
- Merriweather, a steward and veteran who served under Jack
- Dr Gifford, ship's doctor with a taste for sleuthing
- Sam, a cabin boy
- Assorted stewards and shop assistants

CHAPTER ONE

November, 1931

The hand caressed the small bottle like a cherished friend. It had been a while since its last appearance in a little play staged in the cause of fairness. Now, the arsenic would be a welcome travel companion. There were too many rats lurking around wherever one looked. No matter how many legs they had.

The ship horn's blast pierced the early morning silence of Port Adelaide. Frances Palmer's hand slipped into Uncle Sal's as they turned a corner and caught their first sight of the *SS Empress of the Sea*.

The gleaming white ship dwarfed the tugboats on the next pier. Tiny figures swarmed over the deck. The gangway was lowered, ready for the first passengers to come aboard. Frances wondered how many people would travel with them. The ocean liner appeared big enough to house a small town.

Her head whirred as they moved closer. It seemed incredible that for the next six weeks or so this would be their home, and twenty-three-year old Frances Palmer, who'd never been further than Melbourne, would travel half-way around the world to London.

Uncle Sal, who in his glory days as Vaudeville artist Salvatore the Magnificent had played the stages in a dozen countries, eyed the ship with admiration. 'That's a sweet berth we're sailing on,' he said. 'See the elegant lines, with the sheer curve of the hull and that rounded stern? And did you notice how the funnel is placed directly between the two masts?'

'She is a beaut,' Frances agreed, despite her lack of nautical knowledge.

'She's fast, too,' a low voice behind her said.

'Jack.' Frances spun around to find herself enveloped in the arms of Jack Sullivan, owner of the Top Note, Adelaide's finest night club. And, although she had to pinch herself to believe it, he was her fiancé and the reason they were here. Jack's mother in England had begged him to come to her aid for some unspecified reason, and he'd invited Frances and Uncle Sal to come along. They'd work off their passage as Salvatore the Magnificent and his plucky assistant, Signorina Francesca, although Frances had her suspicions that being part of the ship's entertainment would not cover all their expenses.

It would be churlish to probe. This was Uncle Sal's and her dream, to perform together. Uncle Sal's proper career had ended with a car accident that left him with a gammy ankle, and Frances worked as a telephone exchange operator to support herself, her mother, and Uncle Sal. He was her godfather, not her real uncle, and apart from Jack the most sophisticated and lovable man she'd ever met.

He never complained about the change in his circumstances, or the hardship the Great Depression meant for everyone. For now, though, the lack of money in people's pockets allowed Frances to leave her employment for six months. When they returned to Adelaide, her boss had promised she could come back to her switchboard. In her absence, instead of employing a new girl, the other operators would divide up her hours between them.

Jack pushed a lock out of Frances's eyes. 'Ready?' His gaze flickered to her trunk. It was half-empty, despite holding all her presentable clothes. With only a few days' notice, there had been no time to go shopping.

If Frances was honest, she also didn't want to spend any of her hard-earned shillings on clothes that might seem fashionable in South Australia but be considered dowdy in London.

England! Her heart drummed against her ribs. She'd be in London for a winter Christmas and all the magic that entailed.

She wished her mother were here, to see Frances step onto the gleaming gangway with its handrails shining so white they reflected the summer sun. But then Frances would have felt obliged to stay home whereas now, she was free of any obligation. Her mother was happy up in Queensland, helping her son and daughter-in-law preparing for the birth of their second child.

An elegant young couple stepped out of one of the

buildings where passengers could wait. The woman had a fur stole around her shoulders, despite the day already heating up. Her hair shone black like a magpie's wing and her dress could have come straight out of a fashion magazine. Her dapper companion was dressed all in white. He took her arm as she stalked away on her high heels. Behind them followed an older woman with a fur coat slung around her shoulders. Her dark hair showed no traces of silver. Frances suspected an expensive hairdresser deserved the credit for that,

Three porters struggled in their wake, lugging trunks and carpet bags.

Frances glanced at her own outfit of green skirt and yellow jumper. Maybe she should have dressed up, too. Uncle Sal's suit had shiny patches, but his posture would always be dignified. As for Jack, he looked perfectly at ease in his flannels, shirt and lightweight blazer.

'Is it going to be all elegant folks?' she asked.

'Not likely,' Jack said. 'You meet all kinds of people on these voyages. And don't forget, being rich doesn't make them any better than anyone else, only less likely to worry about their bills.'

He signalled a couple of porters to pick up their luggage. 'Shall we?'

Frances slipped her arm through Jack and Uncle Sal's. 'I'm ready for anything.'

They strolled up the gangway at an easy pace. Frances would have loved to race aboard, but it would have been embarrassing to behave childishly in public view, and she didn't want Uncle Sal to make a wrong step.

She broke into a huge smile she couldn't stop. Neither

did she want to. What did it matter if other people realised that she wasn't used to adventures like this? Jack's Top Note was a classy joint, but the *Empress of the Sea* oozed money and an old-world elegance, born of centuries of knowing the Empire's place in the world. Australia couldn't compete with that.

Clacking high heels and giggles behind them announced more arrivals. 'Excuse me,' a high-pitched soprano said behind Frances. She obliged and let go of Jack's arm as she stepped as close to the handrail as possible.

Three young women in fashionable dresses rushed past, leaving behind a trail of too sweet perfume.

'They must be part of the crew,' Uncle Sal said knowingly as he cast an expert eye over the trio who now rushed past a man in uniform.

'They are very smart.' Frances suppressed a little sigh.

'Not as smart as you,' Jack said. 'They probably meant to impress the few locals out and about at this hour.'

He grinned at Frances as he fished a thick envelope with their tickets out of his pocket.

'Good morning, sir.' The uniformed man clicked his heels together and took the papers. 'Mr Sullivan, Miss Palmer, Mr Bernardo. If you'd follow the stewards to your cabins?'

'Thanks,' Jack said, but the man already switched his attention to the next passenger, a dowager-like lady with a nervous corgi in her arms and a mild-mannered young man at her heels.

Inside, the ship was at least as impressive as from the outside. Thick, blue carpet muffled their steps, and the wood gleamed in the light from the glass-domed wall lamps. The porters led them down a flight of stairs that forked off into two directions. They took the left passage, which was flanked by cabin doors. The first steward, carrying Frances' trunk, stopped outside cabin number 107. He unlocked it and stepped aside to allow Frances to enter.

'We'll see you in ten minutes on the promenade deck,' Jack said, as he and Uncle Sal were led further down the passage.

A huge weight dropped off Frances's shoulders as she saw how neat, yet small her cabin was. It consisted of a bed with a trundle bed underneath, a small table, two chairs, a dresser with mirror and a small, inbuilt wardrobe. A door led to a snug bathroom she had to share with the cabin next door.

'Everything alright, Miss?' the steward asked as he showed her around. His Adam's apple bobbed up and down, and he could be no more then seventeen or eighteen, she estimated.

'It's lovely,' she said. 'If you could tell me how to find the promenade deck, I'll leave you to your job.'

He opened the dresser drawer and handed her a stiff, gilt-edged brochure. 'Here's a map of the *Empress*, Miss. For the promenade deck you just follow the passage to the staircase on the starboard side.'

Frances gave him a blank stare.

'That's the left side,' he said. 'Then you go up three flights, and you can't miss it.' He saluted and left her.

She would unpack later, she decided. For now, a quick brush would have to do if she wanted to be punctual.

As she made her way to the promenade deck, brisk

stewards and stewardesses hurried past. Low voices behind the cabin doors reminded her of the fact that she'd spent the voyage in the company of hundreds of travellers. People, who might see Frances Palmer during the day without having any inkling that the ravishing, blonde-wigged Signorina Francesca, who'd perform her act as Salvatore the Magnificent's assistant two nights a week, was the same person.

She chuckled. This was heaven.

CHAPTER TWO

Jack slipped the lanky boy a ten-shilling note as soon as he had deposited the trunk and carpet bag.

The boy grinned so wide his face almost split. 'I'll come back and unpack for you later, sir.'

'That's not necessary but thank you.'

'The name is Sam, sir. In case you need anything.' Judging from his awed tone, the second-class passengers probably didn't dip too freely into their pockets, at least not at the start of a journey when it made most sense to make friends with the people responsible for your comfort.

'Have you been at sea long?' Jack asked.

'It's my second voyage. My uncle's looking after the real toffs in first class.' The boy broke off, panic in his eyes. 'Sorry, sir. I meant no disrespect.'

'No harm done. Don't let me keep you.'

Two knocks on the inside door of their shared bathroom told Jack that Uncle Sal was ready to go up to the promenade deck.

They arrived a minute before Frances. The first passengers already set up claiming their spots on the deck chairs which were lined up with a good view of the sea, or in this case, the pier. The whole promenade deck was covered by a glass roof, and heaters would no doubt make it a pleasant place when they reached the cold parts of the world.

Glass tubes led all the way up to the roof and down into the bowels of the ship, sending the day light into the lower decks, an ingenious system that to Frances was the most ingenious thing she'd ever seen.

'Shall we stroll around?' Jack asked Frances.

'You two enjoy yourself,' Uncle Sal said. 'I'll stick to one of these chairs for a bit. Never had those before on my travels.'

'It's a bit fancier than my last ocean voyage,' Jack agreed. He'd volunteered as soon as the Great War broke out and returned to Australia on one of the first troop ships back home in January 1919.

'She's a corker alright.' Uncle Sal lowered himself into a deck chair and tilted his face up to the sun.

Frances stood transfixed. Outside, a group of people dressed like Hollywood stars were trailed by a gaggle of what must be maids and manservants, laden with baggage. A few steps behind them came porters, with yet more trunks.

Jack was impressed, too. He whistled through his teeth. 'Seems like all the nabobs in the whole of Australia are here in Adelaide.'

'Pardon me.' Frances felt herself nudged aside as a tall young man with pomaded hair strode past, with the dog they'd spotted earlier, straining on his leash. The bejewelled collar sparkled like a Christmas tree. The young man gave her an apologetic smile. 'Tinkerbell here needs a spot of privacy.'

His British accent made Frances curious. Sure enough, most of the smart passengers she'd noticed so far appeared too well-groomed and rich for Adelaide, which, as much as she loved it, was still only a small outpost in a country removed from almost everything. But she'd expected their fellow travellers to be mostly Australians, setting off from Sydney and Melbourne, or New Zealanders.

The *Empress of the Sea* had originally embarked from Lyttelton, and they'd stop in Colombo and Bombay before they reached London. The names alone made Frances's heart ache with longing to see them. If the weather caused no big delays, they should have a whole day to explore each city.

'Would you like a refreshment? I'm thirsty.' Jack touched her back. 'If the bars are already open.'

As if on cue, a waiter with a tray held high in his hands came through the doors at the end of the promenade deck.

A greying man regally snapped his fingers at the waiter who hurried over to serve him and his companion. Both men had aquiline features and bushy eyebrows, so Frances took them to be brothers.

Jack approached the waiter. 'Is it possible to find tea or lemonade somewhere?'

The greying man gave him a contemptuous glare. Jack ignored it.

'The bar in the restaurant one flight down is open,' the

waiter said. 'The other amenities will only be available from noon onwards.'

'I'll join you.' Uncle Sal nimbly climbed out of the chair.

Frances heard the man mutter to his brother, 'Those are the night club folks,' as they followed Uncle Sal and Jack with a haughty stare.

She lifted her chin higher. Jack, who employed as many of the soldiers who'd served under his command as he could afford, and who supported soup kitchens and orphanages, was worth a lot more than these jokers would ever be. The same went for Uncle Sal. And the Top Note was a place to be proud of. It gave people joy, and happiness, and it fed the staff and everyone else remotely involved with it.

'All alone? You're much to pretty for that.' A portly, middle-aged man moved close enough to brush her elbow. She inched away. His hair pomade smelt cloying, and his breath stank of cigar smoke.

'I'm waiting for my uncle, and my fiancé,' she said, hoping he'd get the hint. His gaze flickered to her ringless fingers. For once she cursed herself for keeping her engagement ring safe in her trunk. She didn't want to risk losing it when she had to take it off for her rehearsals, or worse, tempting a loose-fingered person.

She might come from a law-abiding family, but her uncle in Melbourne was a policeman, and since meeting Jack she'd had more than her share of risky adventures.

The portly man inched closer.

Slowly, but firmly she trod on his foot.

He yelped and moved away.

'Everything alright?' Trust Jack to appear in the right moment.

'Absolutely.' She took the lemonade he handed her.

'I'd raise a glass to our voyage, but not with that stuff,' he said.

They left Uncle Sal swilling his beer and reading the newspaper and explored the ship.

There were a few rooms open only for the first-class passengers. If the rest was anything to go by, they must be palatial, Frances thought. The library alone with its reading tables and thick carpets reminded her of a glossy magazine. The shelves were stacked with enough books to keep the keenest reader happy for a lifetime.

Hidden from her sight, inside the writing room a man said, 'I've made a mistake. You must believe me.' The voice had a theatrical tremolo.

Frances wondered if they'd stumbled into an impromptu rehearsal as Jack led her away, to give whoever it was privacy.

The next room pulled a much bigger crowd than the deserted library. Ice-cubes clanked in two cocktail shakers, and a slim bartender in a white uniform studded with brass buttons added splashes of liquor in all colours of the rainbow.

The first drink went to the dowager-like lady Frances had spotted earlier. 'A Monkey Gland for madam,' the bartender said.

The orange-red cocktail shimmered in its glass. Frances eyed it appreciatively. She rarely touched liquor, but this one smelt heavenly of orange juice and grenadine, and she liked the name.

Madam inhaled the aroma before she took a tiny sip.

The small dog shot yapping into the room, dragging the sheepish looking young man behind her. Tinkerbell promptly squatted on his haunches and gazed at his owner.

'Sorry, Aunt Mildred.' The young man mopped his forehead with a monogrammed handkerchief. 'Tink got a bit upset with all the strangers around.'

He signalled the bartender for another Monkey Gland.

'One moment, sir.' The bartender prepared more drinks for a group of young men who lounged in a group of armchairs covered on brown leather. 'Sidecars for Mr Sanders and Mr Fitch, Gin Rickeys for Mr Callahan and Mr Brown.'

He addressed Jack as he mixed the Monkey Gland. 'What can I do for you, sir and madam?'

'One moment,' Aunt Mildred said. 'My nephew will have plain soda water.' A dangerous glint came into her eyes. 'Won't you, Tommy? Drinking alcohol before the cocktail hour is a ruinous habit in a young man and I will not support it.' She patted her dog's head as she reached for her glass.

The young men snickered as Tommy humbly accepted his soda water.

'We'll have soda as well,' Jack said.

'You don't look like a teetotaller.' Mr Fitch, who sported a too bright yellow waistcoat and a thin moustache that could not divert from his weak chin, sneered at Jack.

Jack ignored him.

Aunt Mildred fumbled for the pince-nez attached to her jacket by a thin golden chain and inspected Jack. Tinkerbell sidled up to him and rubbed himself against Jack's leg.

'You appear to be a sensible man,' she said. 'And my dog approves of you. Tinkerbell is never wrong.'

'I try.' Jack's expression was solemn.

'I wish I could say the same about most of the young generation.'

Tommy opened his mouth to protest but thought better of it. Frances felt a surge of pity for him. He must be at least twenty-seven, she thought, and despite his round face and pink cheeks he looked like a rugby player, not someone who cowered before a relative. Unless of course, she held the purse-strings.

'Not the sense God gave a goose.' Aunt Mildred emptied her cocktail. 'Mind you, my dear late brother was as bad. A pretty face, a sad story, and he'd open his pocket-book.'

'I say, Aunt Mildred.' Tommy loosened his suddenly too tight collar.

'Shush, my boy. You're lucky your mother made up for your father's failings.' She spoke to Jack again, without bothering to include Frances. Maybe she hadn't seen her, Frances thought charitably. The dim light in the cocktail bar and the obvious near-sightedness of Aunt Mildred would explain that.

'I won't ask you to keep an eye on my boy, but –'

The young men now snickered openly. She quelled them with one glance. 'At least my nephew is worth caring about, which is obviously more than can be said about you lot. Bright young things? Good riddance to that.'

'Hold it.' Mr Fitch's already flushed face grew redder.

Mr Brown, a reedy youngster with a signet ring and protruding teeth, put a calming hand on Mr Fitch's shoulder. 'Leave the old bird alone and let's have another drink.'

Aunt Mildred harrumphed, swept up Tinkerbell in her arms and sailed out of the room, Tommy in her wake.

'What are you staring at?' asked Mr Fitch of nobody in particular.

Frances had finished her soda water. Giving the bartender a sympathetic shrug, she signalled to Jack she was ready to go.

The doors to the ball room where they'd perform were still closed, but they found Tommy gazing at it longingly. His redoubtable aunt was nowhere in sight. Only Tinkerbell could be heard, yapping away in the powder room further down the passage.

Tommy spun around as he heard them nearing. He seemed to be awfully nervy, Frances thought, although his open face and admiring glance endeared him to her.

'Awfully sorry about the scene in the bar,' he said. 'My aunt Mildred is an awful good sort once you get to know her better.'

'No worries.' Jack held out his hand. 'Jack Sullivan, and this is my fiancée, Miss Palmer.'

Tommy shook Jack's hand with abandon. 'She's not usually taking to the giggle water this early, only before we're going out to sea. It calms her insides.'

'I'm not judging,' Jack said. 'Before you ask, I'm not a wowser either. I only prefer to wait until the sun's over the yardarm.'

'Right, right.' Tommy ruffled his hair. 'I'm forgetting my manners. Tommy Clifton.'

From inside the ballroom came soft voices. 'They're cleaning up,' Tommy said. 'Have you had a peek inside yet?'

'We only came aboard this morning,' Frances said. 'But I've seen pictures.'

'We saw you, didn't we, when we returned to the ship? Aunt Mildred likes to spend a night on the town when we can.'

'You stayed in Adelaide overnight? Anywhere special?' Frances asked.

Tommy craned his neck towards the powder room and lowered his voice. 'The Grosvenor Hotel. Not a bad old place.'

Not a bad old place? Frances had to stop her jaw from dropping. The four-storey hotel on North Terrace with its marble façade attracted only the wealthiest of guests.

'Not much of a night on the town,' Jack said.

Tommy's pink cheeks went a little redder. 'When Auntie was asleep, I went for a stroll and found a smashing little place. The Top Note. That singer they have ...' He broke of as if only now remembering Frances. 'Have you been there?'

'Oh, yeah.' Frances gave a little shrug. 'Not a bad old place, eh, Jack?'

'I've seen worse.' Jack gave her a wink. 'I assume you don't want anyone else to know?'

'Know what?' Aunt Mildred and Tinkerbell were surprisingly light on their feet. Tommy gave a start. His eyes bulged.

'That your nephew enjoyed his stay in our fair city very much. It wouldn't endear him to the Sydneysiders or

Melbournians on this ship.' Jack flashed her a disarming smile.

Aunt Mildred snorted. 'We're not in the business of endearing ourselves to people.'

'I thought so. We'll see you two later.' Jack chuckled to himself as they left their new acquaintances behind.

A shudder ran through the ship as the engines started.

The horn blasted. 'We're ready to leave port,' Jack said. 'Shall we wave Adelaide farewell from the observation deck?'

CHAPTER THREE

Frances's heart pounded as she clung to the railing. Luckily, Jack and Uncle Sal shielded her from the throng that pushed ever closer, to wave their hats to the people on shore. The horn blared again, and at a distance, another ship answered in a joyous toot. Smoke puffed up from the funnels as the *Empress* juddered to life. They were officially at sea.

The ship left its berth at a crawl, until it was clear of Adelaide's port, before it picked up speed. The sudden change surprised Frances. She planted her feet wide to stay balanced, as Uncle Sal had taught her.

Next to her, a young blonde in a sleeveless gown was less fortunate. She fell back, only to be caught by a young swell.

'Well played by that little sheila,' Uncle Sal whispered to Frances. Indeed, the blonde simpered and thanked her hero so profusely he offered to buy her tea or something stronger, to steady her nerves.

All around the, the crowd thinned. 'Ready for lunch?' Jack asked as a steward beckoned them.

'I'm not that hungry. Do you think I could get a sandwich instead?' Frances hated to tear herself away from the view. She wouldn't see Adelaide again for six months and wanted to memorise every inch of it.

'That shouldn't be a problem.' Jack joined the steward, who busily checked off names on an endless seeming list.

'Jack Sullivan, party of three,' he said.

'That's with Mr Sal Bernardo and Miss Frances Palmer?' The steward checked again. 'We have you down for the second setting at lunch and dinner at eight.'

'Good-oh. But is there anywhere we can have a snack instead of a full lunch?'

The steward glanced up. A faint scar on the clean-shaven chin marred his regular features, but like most of the crew, he might have been chosen for his looks as well as his professional skills, with his glossy straw-coloured hair and broad shoulders. 'Why, it's Captain Jack Sullivan!' He clapped Jack on the shoulder, before he caught himself. 'Sorry, sir.'

Jack grinned. 'Nice to see you too, Sergeant Merriweather.'

'Bluey not with you?'

'He and his missus are keeping the business ticking over while I'm gone.'

'Get a bustle on, mate,' someone behind them said.

The steward sprang to attention. 'If you'd like to go the piano bar, you'll find everything you need.'

'Is there any place where you don't run into old

acquaintances?' Frances asked as they left the observation deck.

'It's always good to have someone on the inside.' Jack chuckled. 'Good old Merry.'

'One of your men?' Uncle Sal led them unerringly to the piano bar. Frances suspected he'd studied the plan of the *Empress of the Sea* well enough to find his way around blindfolded. Including the way to the lifeboats. Although this was Frances's first proper trip, he'd drilled it into her years ago to make sure she acquainted herself first thing with fire escapes and emergency exits in any place she went.

Soft music tinkled in the piano bar. A small man with melancholy eyes played for the dozen people who'd also shunned the dining room and opted for lighter refreshment instead.

Frances was surprised by the number of empty glasses on the tables. 'That's a lot of daytime drinking,' she said.

'Some people like to make up for the limitations they face on land,' Jack said. 'But the crew will make sure folks don't go blotto. They're good at that.'

'As good as you?' Regulars at the Top Note were well aware that although champagne and liquor flowed freely, drunken shenanigans were not tolerated. Grogged-up customers would be sent home with a cabbie. Here, the crew would probably bundle them into their cabins.

'I'd guess so. But whatever happens, it's not my business. For once, I'll enjoy myself with you two and not care about anything else.'

Uncle Sal ordered tea and sandwiches for three. 'Hear,

hear,' he said. 'Here's to fun times ahead and a quiet and peaceful life.'

Jack changed into evening dress and mused about the day. Fancy running into old Merry. He'd have to tell him to keep it quiet that Jack ran a nightclub. Otherwise people would either snub him and his companions, or cozy up to him in the hope he'd bring some excitement into their dull existence.

He intended to do nothing of that sort. Instead, he'd watch Uncle Sal and Frances perform, dance with his darling girl, and when she and Uncle Sal were rehearsing or otherwise occupied, he'd take out his sketch books.

He didn't keep many secrets, but one was the desire to paint again. First the war and then the responsibilities he shouldered had put paid to his dreams of studying to become a painter. It was all well and dandy to be a hungry artist on his own. When you had a sister and mother and his old soldiers to support though, things no longer worked like that. He'd never turn his back on them, but a long sea voyage to sketch and paint was perfect for him. Until they docked in London, he'd only be Jack Sullivan, man of leisure.

Frances twisted her torso to close the small buttons on the side of her dress. It was made of cotton, not silk, but it fit like a glove, and the soft blue matched her eyes. White gloves and a small evening clutch she'd purchased in a used clothes shop completed her finery. She powdered her nose and swiped on a layer of dark pink lipstick.

Fancy that only a week ago, she'd sat on her chair at the telephone exchange and afterwards come home to tackle the cooking and cleaning with Uncle Sal's help. That seemed a lifetime away for the new Frances Palmer, lady of leisure. It wouldn't last, but while it did, she'd make the most of it. No problems to solve, or tasks to perform other than standing on stage with Uncle Sal.

She sashayed out of her cabin and nearly tripped over Tinkerbell's leash. The dog sat down and scratched his neck where a fly tickled him.

'I say, are you okay?' Tommy peered at her in obvious concern. 'I'm frightfully sorry, but Tink has a mind of his own.'

'No harm done,' she said. 'Where's your aunt?'

'Getting ready for dinner.' He pulled a face. 'We're actually along the next passage, but Tink likes this way. He has a few favourite spots here, like the one behind the stairway.'

Tommy swooped up the dog as he fell into step with her. 'Better make sure this little rascal doesn't trip up more people.'

Tink's ears twitched, and Frances could have sworn the little dog grinned at her. 'You're his dog-sitter? That can't be too much fun.'

'I don't mind. Sometimes Auntie hands Tink over to a steward he's taken a shine on, and after dinner he stays in his basket in her cabin. He's a cute little guy, actually.' He ruffled Tink's head. 'So's Aunt Mildred. Although she's not a guy, but a gal, and a pretty sporting one.'

Frances thought back at the patronising behaviour the sporting gal had shown towards her nephew. Well, each to their own.

He grinned. 'I know what you're thinking, but she's only trying to protect me. Not that any gold-digger would be interested in my empty pockets. Still, she means well, and there have been a few incidents happening to friends of mine with a certain type of gal.'

He stopped himself. 'I shouldn't have said that, should I? I'm making an ass of myself, again.'

Frances laughed. 'Not at all.'

Tink wriggled out of Tommy's arms and hid under the stairway where he ran in tiny circles until he was dizzy.

Frances crouched to watch the happy little dog. 'Does he do that every time?'

'Without fail. He also loves running off with the discs for shuffleboard, and his favourite hiding spot is in the laundry basket in my room.'

Tink picked himself up again and started another round of running.

'He'll go on for a bit. Don't wait on our account,' Tommy said. 'Toodle-ooh.'

Frances chuckled to herself. Tommy and his aunt sounded exactly like they did in the novels by P.G. Wodehouse she'd taken out from the public library in preparation for her trip. Her best friend Pauline had recommended them, to prepare Frances for London society. Until today, she'd never thought people really talked like that.

She swept off to meet Jack and Uncle Sal, ready for her great adventure.

Fleet-footed waiters weaved their way through the dining-room, trays held at eye-level. Frances marvelled at their agility. Acres of white tablecloth shimmered in the light of chandeliers and crystal glasses clinked.

A waiter showed them to their table, close to the dance floor and the stage where a string-quartet played a fox-trot. Frances glanced around under her eyelashes. First and second-class passengers seemed to be mixed, judging by their appearance. Some of the women wore what would amount to a king's ransom around their necks and wrists. Among them were the two fur-clad ladies that had boarded with them. They could have walked straight out of a fashion magazine with their silk frocks, diamond earrings and bracelets sparkling on black opera gloves.

Did they wear them while eating? P.G. Wodehouse had delivered no clues to that part of upper crust etiquette. What marred their elegance though was the light contempt as the women regarded their neighbours. Their male companion did not sneer, but his gaze wandered around restlessly until it lit upon a slender young redhead. The girl joined a table where the blonde, who'd stumbled so artistically earlier, and a brunette were half through their meal.

The older woman produced a folded silk fan of the kind the China Store sold and rapped the man lightly over his knuckles. 'Please do pay attention to your fiancée, Lawrence. Dear Rosalie asked you to signal the waiter for our champagne.'

That knuckle-rap could have come straight out of a novel, Frances thought.

'Anything amusing?' Jack asked. 'You're miles away.'

'People gazing,' she admitted. 'I feel a bit like an intruder.'

'Nonsense, my darling.' Uncle Sal beckoned the waiter. 'I'll have the soup, roast chicken, and apple pie for dessert.'

'The same for me,' said Frances. Jack ordered salad and steak and the apple pie as well.

The food was done to perfection, with the chicken skin crisp and the white flesh so tender it fell off the bone.

Frances forced herself to slow down and savour every bite. The last thing she wanted was to appear greedy, or ill-mannered.

'We'll sit here, thank you very much.' Aunt Mildred, resplendent in a fur-trimmed evening gown and with diamond clips holding up her silver curls, put her evening clutch on Frances's table. She waved the steward away who attempted to steer her towards a bigger, better placed table. The poor man had no choice but to give in and pull out chairs at Frances's table for the newcomers. The last chair was for Tink whose tongue lolled out as he sniffed the chicken.

'You don't mind, do you?' Tommy asked Jack who gave him a reaffirming shrug.

'Why should they?' Aunt Mildred snapped her fingers at the steward. 'Kindly make sure your colleague will take Tinkerbell for a stroll after he's eaten.'

Jack petted Tink. 'I'd offer you a bite, mate, but I'm not sure what you have for your dinner.'

'A morsel of that chicken will do nicely. If one of you would be so kind?'

Frances cut off a piece and put it on a plate the steward placed on the chair with Tink. The little dog groaned with delight as he devoured it.

His doting mistress beamed at Frances. 'Isn't he darling?'

She turned to Uncle Sal. 'We haven't been properly introduced yet. I'm Mrs Walter Clifton, the Right Honourable Walter Clifton, but please call me Mildred. You've met my nephew Tommy.'

Uncle Sal bowed over her hand. 'Delighted. I'm Salvatore –'

'Bernardo, the Magnificent.' It must have been a trick of the light that made her face appear flushed for an instant.

Up close, Frances estimated her to be younger than she originally thought. She couldn't be much older than Uncle Sal.

'I recognised you straight away, from your days at the Alhambra in London. You haven't changed at all.'

Uncle Sal inclined his head. 'You flatter me.'

'When I was young it was my dream to tread the boards myself. Impossible for a young lady of my class, of course, but at least I could sneak into the music halls and theatres.' Her eyes took on a dreamy expression.

Uncle Sal smoothed his pencil-thin moustache. 'Halcyon days, my dear lady. That smell of grease-paint, the cheers from the audience.' He sighed. 'Vaudeville had its day, and so did I.'

The steward brought two silver-domed trays with salad and more chicken for Aunt Mildred and Tommy.

They'd barely started when Merry, the steward, arrived to take charge of Tink.

The little dog greeted him with a happy wag of its stubby tail. 'Off you go with our friend, Tinkerbell.' Aunt Mildred pressed a kiss on the silky head. 'You won't forget to bring him to my cabin, won't you, Merriweather?'

'Indeed not, Mrs Clifton. Come along, Tink.'

'They're such good friends,' Aunt Mildred said as she blew her dog a last kiss. 'So important to have people you can rely on. Tommy does his best, but the dear boy does deserve a bit of freedom.'

She fell silent as she enjoyed her meal. Only after coffee had been served did she say, 'Why don't you young people enjoy yourselves while Mr Bernardo and I chat.'

'Sal, for you.' Was he flirting a little?

Frances had no time to pay more attention to Uncle Sal and his admirer, because Jack led her to the dance floor. For a few blissful moments she lost herself in the sounds of "Dream A Little Dream of Me" and the warmth of Jack's arms.

An elbow brought her out of her reverie.

Lawrence, with Rosalie as his partner, had done a misstep and bumped into Frances.

His fiancée glared at him before plastering on a sweet smile.

The red-haired girl he'd watched earlier, glided past in the arms of a rotund gentleman old enough to be her father. Her dress was fashionable and would have fooled anyone who wasn't used to cheap materials herself, like Frances.

Her blonde friend was draped around the swell she'd flirted with earlier.

The brunette danced close-by, with another man rich in money and years.

Frances admired the ease with which they made graceless men appear graceful. Her own dancing skills were no match. Neither were Tommy's, who swung helplessly in the arms of a muscular matron.

'They're professional dancers.' Jack twirled Frances out of Lawrence's way. 'A few of the men are staff members as well. Can you spot them?'

By now the dance floor heaved with couples and Frances felt the heat. She wished the ceiling fans would be switched on. 'Do you mind if we take a break? I could do with some fresh air.'

They slipped away, past the red-head who watched Lawrence's retreating back with a sad expression, while her partner trod on her feet. A pang of pity hit Frances. She knew only too well how easy it was to fall in love with a man much wealthier and sophisticated than oneself.

Jack let Uncle Sal know where to find them. Frances fanned herself. As an already too familiar voice behind her told Rosalie to have Lawrence show her the stars, she stepped in the opposite direction. On her first night on the ocean, she wanted nothing to diminish her and Jack's happiness, and company would definitely spoil that. Especially the wrong one.

A tipsy man swayed across the deck, singing to himself. 'Ladidah.'

He collided with Jack who steadied him.

'Sorry, mate,' the man mumbled.

Jack still held him by the arms. 'That's alright,' he said in an amused tone that made the hairs on Frances's arms stand up.

'Steward?'

Merriweather came into view.

'Can you help this gentleman to his cabin? And make sure he's well looked after?' Jack handed the man over and grimaced. 'Silly me. I forgot to mention I do want my wallet back first.'

He slipped his hand into the man's jacket and pulled out three wallets. 'Maybe you should have a chat with your security officer, steward. And do a proper search.'

He took Frances's arm and strolled away, leaving Merriweather to deal with the squirming pickpocket who'd dropped all pretence of being drunk.

CHAPTER FOUR

The waves lapped against the ships hull, no more than a mere whisper on the observation desk. The stars glittered in the night sky and sparked tiny flashes on the water. Jack draped his jacket over Frances's shoulders. Dotted all over the space, couples strolled around in the dim light from the lamps. A few deckchairs were taken despite the late hour as people drank in the romance of the night.

Back home, at this hour the Top Note would be humming, with people waiting for Dolores Barden to sing. Or for Jack to have a chat. Only they wouldn't be able to find him.

Frances wondered if Bluey and his wife Marie really could take care of everything the way Jack did. As wonderful as it was to be here, and travelling, with Jack at her side, it didn't bear thinking about any problems at the club. It meant too much to Jack, and to all her friends.

'What's going to happen now?' she asked, thinking back to the pickpocket.

'Now we enjoy the stars and our freedom, and then we'll dance again until you're tired.' Jack's teeth flashed white in the twilight.

'With that man you handed over to Merry. Aren't we a long way from our next port?'

'They'll probably stow him away safely until they can let the police have him. Thefts are taken seriously on ships. If passengers don't believe in their safety, it's bad for business.'

'But how can you steal with nobody noticing?'

Jack shrugged. 'We had one clever joker at the Top Note who'd return the wallet with a few quid less. Hard to keep track of your expenses when you're getting sozzled. Or you drop it somewhere for a steward to find.'

'Would Bluey have spotted a pickpocket?'

He cupped her chin. 'You worry too much. Bluey has enough troops to soldier on, and you've seen his wife in action. Don't forget there's Dolores's boyfriend too. You'd have to be stupid to pull a fast one in a place where police are regulars.'

Frances had to admit that was true. Because the only law the Top Note broke was the six pm alcohol ban, the club proved popular with high-ranking police officers, councillors and other influential people. On top of that, Dolores's beau was a police detective, who could be counted on to come to their rescue. He also was the Palmer's lodger. Without his rent, and the additional income from another lodger Jack had sent them, she wouldn't have been able to afford this voyage and pay the mortgage in her family home.

Jack said, 'If there is anything Bluey needs help with, they'll send me a telegram. I told you, it's all under control.'

She snuggled against him. He was right, all was well with her world.

The red-head and her brunette friend came through the doors and stopped three yards from Jack and Frances. Their former dance partners hung back and lit foul-smelling cigars.

'You play your cards right and you'll be in clover,' the brunette said. She spun around and waved at the men. 'Your sugar daddy has the hots for you.'

'I'm not interested. I do my job, that's all.'

'Evie, please don't tell me it's still about that Lawrence Vaughan.'

The red-head took out a silver cigarette case she must have kept hidden in her clothes. She struck a match and lit a gasper.

'Butt me?' The brunette helped herself to a cigarette. She narrowed her eyes to keep the smoke out of it as she blew rings.

'For your information, Mr Vaughan means nothing to me. He's just another passenger,' Evie said.

'That's good, because he'll soon be manacled for good to that Rosalie broad. Her mama will see to that.' The girl took the cigarette case and ran her finger over the engraved swirls. A red gem decorated the clasp. 'At least he gave you a nice present.'

'I told you it was nothing.' Evie walked over to a table with an ashtray and stubbed out her cigarette. 'Come on, Nancy. Break's over.'

As soon as Evie and Nancy were gone with their dance partners, a trio of men Frances took to be merchants or successful farmers, took their place. Their tweed suits had that rough quality that set working men's clothes apart from the hunting attire of the upper classes.

Frances giggled. Mr Wodehouse's novels really were an education in themself. She'd never made this kind of observation before. One of the best things about Australia, in her opinion the best place in the world, was its lack of a class system. An immigrant like Uncle Sal or Jack was as good as a descendent of the first fleet, and a telephone exchange operator like Frances held the same place as the wife of a governor.

Jack always was quick to point out that this classlessness only encompassed white people, even if their forebears were convicts, but he admitted it was better than most systems.

England on the other hand was enthralled with lords and ladies and people who called each other "old prune" and were raised by an army of nannies and valets. A girl like Evie, who worked for a living, was as good as anyone in Australia. In England, she'd be a nobody.

'Another dance?'

Frances expected they'd return to the dining room, but instead Jack led her to a ball room with stained-glass ceilings, gold-trimmed lamps and two bars with tables on opposite sides of the dance floor.

A band with a proper conductor played the latest hits. Frances's mouth went dry when she realised this was the same stage, she and Uncle Sal would perform on.

Jack swept her into a waltz that seemed over in a heartbeat. The drummer played a drum roll as a spotlight fell on a slender figure, dressed in white satin and with her red hair gleaming.

'Evie?' Frances wasn't even aware she'd said the name out loud when an angry hiss next to her showed not everyone admired the girl.

Frances couldn't see who'd hissed, but whatever annoyed that person, Evie's voice could not be the reason. That, although no match to the star of the Top Note, had just the right amount of innocence and freshness to make listening and dancing to it an equal pleasure.

A few minutes before midnight, Frances's head throbbed from the music, the chatter and the heat of the crowd. With a long sea voyage ahead, she had ample opportunity to have fun in the ball room. Tomorrow, she and Uncle Sal had their first rehearsal on stage. He'd already retired, in preparation for an early morning.

His new-found friend, Aunt Mildred, seemed as bright-eyed as ever as she held Tommy in an iron grip on the dance floor. Tommy rolled his eyes in mock despair at Frances, as she and Jack walked past on their way to their cabins, but he seemed to be cheerful enough.

Frances rubbed her aching feet as she sank into her bunk. She hoped they would have recovered in the morning, because her act demanded of her to be nimble. Afterwards, she intended to explore the *Empress* from stem to stern. She drifted off with a happy expression on her face.

Breakfast turned out to be an important event. Frances had risen early, and she'd expected the breakfast room to be deserted. Instead, the stewards rushed around to refill the carts with toast, porridge, eggs, bacon, kidneys, kippers and kedgeree. She stuck to toast and scrambled eggs, same as Uncle Sal. He'd taught her not to overeat before a rehearsal or a performance.

'Tea or coffee?' Merry asked. She detected a twinkle in his eyes, although his manner was correct to a fault.

'Tea, please.'

'Indian or China? We've got Assam, Darjeeling, Ceylon and Lapsang Souchong.'

Frances nibbled her lip. She could either select the poshest-sounding tea and pretend to be a society lady, or expose herself as what she was, an ordinary girl who wasn't quite a staff member, but also anything but a well-to-do passenger.

She noticed Uncle Sal's amused glance on her. He'd probably encountered this decision on more occasions than he could remember.

Merry opened the tea caddy, ready for her choice.

She made a snap decision. 'You don't happen to have Billy Tea?' she asked. Billy Tea wasn't posh or famous, but it was as honestly Australian as Frances. She had a box in her luggage, wrapped as a present for Jack's mother. She'd hesitated before buying it, but the packaging was so pretty with its picture of a swagman brewing his tea that she couldn't resist.

The twinkle in Merry's eyes intensified. 'I'll see what I can do for you, Miss Palmer.'

'Take a tea-bag out of my box.' Evie gracefully took a seat at the table next to Frances and Uncle Sal, together with her girlfriends. Her fair skin shone as if lit from within, and her face was bare of make-up, in stark contrast to her friends.

'Thank you,' Frances said and introduced herself and Uncle Sal. 'I loved your songs last night.'

'That's swell to hear. I only do a few sets, to give our real singers a break, but it's fun.'

'You're as good as them any day,' Nancy said. 'Isn't that right, Ada?'

The blonde signalled Merry to heap her plate full of egg and bacon. For someone as slender, she had an enormous appetite. 'The bees' knees,' she agreed. 'It's a shame you never got further than the front row of the chorus.'

'The chorus?' Uncle Sal treated the girls to his most charming smile. 'I knew as soon as I clapped eyes on you ladies that you belonged on the boards.'

'Two seasons in the London Pavilion,' Evie said. 'Have you heard of it?'

'One of London's finest musical theatres. I was there in 1921, when Clifton Webb starred in "Fun of the Fayre". I had a small engagement at the Vaudeville Theatre myself.'

'You're that Sal?' Evie nudged Ada, who was too busy tucking into her breakfast to pay any attention. 'Ada, these are the two entertainers that are joining us for this trip.'

Heat rose in Frances's cheeks. 'Uncle Sal is the real deal, but I'm not really an entertainer.'

Uncle Sal wagged a finger at her. 'Oh, yes, you are.

Simply because we only do a few shows, doesn't diminish what you do.'

'Yes, sirree,' Nancy said. 'What do you say, girls, shall we make sure Fran here doesn't miss out on any fun?'

'She didn't do too badly last night.' Ada put her fork aside and chortled. 'Nice looking toff you landed.'

'You mean Jack? He's my ---'

'Fiancé.' Jack gave the girls a nod as he sat down. 'Sorry I'm running late.'

Ada cast an experienced eye over Jack.

Nancy elbowed her. 'Stop it, or people will think you've got no manners.'

Ada pouted, until she broke out in laughter. 'Don't worry, Fran, he's safe from us. Good to know you're out of the competition.'

She waved to another steward, for more tea and toast. Her friends stuck to toast and eggs, like Frances.

Ten minutes later, Frances folded her napkin and put it on her empty plate. She could get used to this, she thought. Good food, her favourite company in the world, and no dishes to clean afterwards.

'Good morning.' Tommy and Aunt Mildred made their way towards them. Tink gave a small welcoming yap from the safety of Aunt Mildred's arms.

'It's unhygienic to allow animals in the dining area. Or the lower classes.' From across the room, Rosalie's mother's voice rose in a stage whisper. Aunt Mildred glowered at her, only to encounter a stare hostile enough to floor a lesser woman.

Evie and Nancy both changed colour. Ada's eyes narrowed to slits. 'Mean old trout.'

'Shh.' Evie touched Ada's arm.

Aunt Mildred swept over to a table already set with a dog bowl under one chair. 'Tommy, dear, please check with the purser on their methods of pest control. We don't want Tinkerbell to catch anything.' Her glance flitted over her opponent.

Tommy's lips twitched. 'Yes, Auntie.'

Merry put two full plates down for them. Obviously, he knew their routine by heart, Frances thought. But then most people were creatures of habit, and a good steward remembered these things.

Aunt Mildred let her pooch out of her arms. He licked her hand. She made little kissing noises until she froze. 'Tommy.'

'Yes?' Tommy stopped his coffee cup halfway to his lips.

Aunt Mildred lifted up Tink and dangled him in the air. 'Look at his collar. He's lost a ruby.'

Coffee sloshed over the side of Tommy's cup. His mouth fell open.

'A missing jewel!' A burly man of military appearance with bushy eyebrows stood up and pointed a finger at Merry. 'Isn't this fellow always running around with your little dog? Those gems must be worth quite a lot for a man in his position.'

Jack stood up, too. 'Are you making any accusations, sir?'

'I'm only saying what's obvious. You're one of those commies that think Jack's as good as his master?'

'Stop it.' Aunt Mildred pressed a hand against her temple. 'You're making a fuss over nothing.'

'More fool you,' the burly man growled. 'Mark my words, your steward has stolen that ruby, and who knows what else he's made off with.' He whistled for another steward. 'Go and tell you captain we've caught a criminal and demand his arrest.'

CHAPTER FIVE

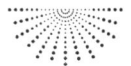

*A*n ashen-faced Merriweather left the room sandwiched between two gloomy sailors. Rosalie's mother went so far as to offer her sympathies to Aunt Mildred who sat here like a statue. Judging by her tone of voice, the woman meant it.

Frances hated having to leave Jack who must be crushed by the accusations against his fellow veteran, but she and Uncle Sal had been hired to do a job, and that included their rehearsals.

The ballroom had that desolate air of places that only came alive in the night. Potpourri masked the staleness, and the ceiling fans would do the rest to freshen the room up for tonight.

The stage too was nothing than a large wooden platform, with a row of spotlights running above.

One of the stewards checked the mechanism of Uncle Sal's wheeled chair which was affixed to the stage with a rod. Within this confinement, it moved freely though, and they'd worked out a routine where Frances would spin the chair around while Uncle Sal juggled. They'd also perform their daring knife-throwing act, with Frances strapped into a wooden frame, acting as target. Because any ship movement would increase the difficulty, they'd made the frame big enough to allow for tiny jerks.

It took all of Frances's willpower to beam brightly throughout the number, although she knew she was safe. Although he had full confidence in Uncle Sal's abilities, Jack had purchased a set of stage knives from the best prop maker in London. They gave off a lethal impression with their sharp blades that caught the light and bone handles. They even appeared to bury themselves into the wood, although the blades retreated into the hilt at the moment of impact. Frances was unsure how they held on to the wood, but they did, perfecting the illusion.

'Frances, sweetheart?' Uncle Sal lowered himself into his chair. 'Are you okay?'

'Sure.' She forced herself to take a deep breath and counted backwards from one hundred.

Uncle Sal braced himself in his seat, focussed only on the items on a table next to Frances. She lowered a gramophone needle onto a record. During the show, they'd have the drummer to keep them in rhythm. While they were rehearsing, a recording would have to do.

'Da-da-dah, da-da-dah,' Frances said under her breath as she flung five red balls as smoothly as she could. The ship moved under her feet, and Uncle Sal struggled to catch two of the balls. She'd have to adjust her aim.

An hour later, both she and Uncle Sal were exhausted

as they traipsed into the dressing room. They had another rehearsal schedule for tomorrow, and they needed it to polish their act. Who could have thought that a tiny shift in the floor under her feet would make such a difference? She'd used different muscles too, to keep her balance.

'We need to find our sea-legs,' Uncle Sal said. 'Blimey if I'd seen that coming.'

'It was alright when I was dancing.' Frances rolled her shoulders and wiggled her toes. She'd clenched them inside her spangly shoes as she stood strapped into the wrist and ankle holds. Her fingernails had painfully dug into her palms a few times as well.

Three short knocks announced Jack. 'Come in, son,' Uncle Sal sang out as he wiped his forehead with a flannel.

'I've brought you some water. You must be parched.' Jack filled two glasses for Frances and Uncle Sal. She gulped her drink down. thankful for the refreshment.

'What happened to Merry?' she asked.

A shutter came down in Jack's face. 'Considering the hullaballoo, the captain had no choice but to have him locked away in a cabin.'

'But surely Mildred would not have stood by idly while your old sergeant was accused.' Uncle Sal smoothed his moustache.

'Doesn't matter what she believes, if something valuable is missing and a gentleman of good standing and his cronies point their fingers at a suspect.' Jack spat the words out.

'You don't believe it.'

'I'd sooner think Aunt Mildred herself had made off with that blasted ruby.'

'Because you were in the war together.' Frances nodded.

'That too, but also because it'd be stupid, and Merry is not a moron.'

'Then what are we waiting for?' Frances made for the door. 'Come on, we have to clear a man's name.'

CHAPTER SIX

'Come in,' Aunt Mildred said. Normally, Frances would have been overawed by the elegance of the two-bedroom suite, with its ankle-deep carpet and furniture straight out of a society magazine. The port hole offered her a glimpse of the foam-crested sea as she took the seat proffered by a pale Tommy.

Aunt Mildred's face set in heavy lines, making her show every day of her age underneath the powder. Only Tinkerbell slept undisturbed in his basket.

Jack and Uncle Sal remained standing until Aunt Mildred had taken her place on the shell-shaped sofa.

'I'm glad you're here,' she said. 'These idiotic officers won't listen to me, and they won't let me see the captain.'

'They can't afford to let Merriweather go,' Jack said. 'Not with their jobs depending on satisfied customers.'

'That's as may be, but still, I say it's utter tosh to suspect Merriweather.'

Jack smiled at her. 'Too right it is. If he'd wanted to steal from you, he'd have waited until we reach London, and made his escape. Stealing anything when we've barely left port is sheer idiocy.'

'Exactly. I've been telling the First Officer, there's not a shred of evidence against the man.' Aunt Mildred snapped her fingers at Tommy.

He picked up the cocktail shaker. 'Would you care for a drink?'

The shock must have shown on Frances's face, because Aunt Mildred chuckled. 'It's only fruit juices, dear. I never touch the hard stuff before the cocktail hour, once we're under way.'

Tink stretched in his sleep and scratched his neck, vaguely reminding Frances of something.

'May I see the collar?' she asked.

Tommy handed it to her.

Jack lowered himself onto the arm of her chair and inspected it with her. The collar was made of the softest silver leather laid in with a dozen evenly spaced rubies and sapphires, fitted in silver. One fitting sat empty, and the leather around it felt rough to the touch.

Frances ran her finger across it.

Jack took the collar and held it up to the light. 'The important question is, did you make everyone believe you put a real bejewelled collar on your little dog, or did someone replace it with one using costume jewellery? Someone like your nephew who had ample opportunity to study the original in detail?'

Tommy spluttered. 'What are you saying?'

'Quiet, my dear.' Aunt Mildred took the collar. 'You're right. I use the copy for voyages like this, Mr Sullivan, precisely to avoid theft.'

'You could have mentioned that when Merriweather was accused of stealing that ruby,' Frances said, oddly disappointed in the old lady.

'It wouldn't have made any difference. To what purpose? For all accounts, the value of the stone doesn't matter. Theft's a crime, no matter if it's only a tuppence,' Jack said.

'If not Merriweather, then who would take it? And why not take the whole collar if you believe it's hugely valuable?' Frances wondered.

'There were scratch marks around the empty setting,' Jack said.

Frances inspected them again. 'Small ones. Like sharp needles or a pincer to pry the fake ruby loose.'

A tiny snore escaped Tink. His paw twitched.

Frances rose and knelt by the basket. 'Tinkerbell?' she whispered. The dog stirred. Frances lifted his paw and stroked it. The toenails were small and sharp.

'I believe I've found our criminal,' she said. 'I've seen Tinkerbell scratch at the collar. If one of the stones wasn't set properly, it could easily have fallen out.'

Jack gave her a resounding kiss. 'That's my girl.'

'It's the only explanation that makes sense, although my darling hardly ever scratches himself,' Aunt Mildred said. 'Yet it won't help poor Merriweather if we don't find the blasted ruby.'

'We'll split up and search for it. The crew hasn't found it yet, or they would have taken it to the chief purser.' Jack gazed around. 'Mrs Clifton – '

'Mildred, please.'

'Mildred, if you and Uncle Sal could search your cabin,

your nephew together with Frances and I will take a geek at Tink's favourite spots.'

They set off, almost colliding with people on their way to lunch.

Uncle Sal and Aunt Mildred stayed behind.

'Do you have a magnifying glass? Or a compact mirror?' Uncle Sal slipped out of his shoes, to the surprise of his hostess.

She opened her purse and took out a powder dose. She set it on the glass table and removed the powder puff. A tiny cloud of grains settled promptly on the table. 'It has a mirror inside.'

'If I use that, it might spread powder all over your lovely cabin. Do you have anything else?' Uncle Sal took a step on his stockinged feet. And another, putting one foot directly in front of the other. 'If we tread on that blimmin' stone with our shoes, we'd never have the foggiest notion with carpet this thick,' he said. 'With bare feet, you'd have to have soles of leather not to feel it.'

'What a clever idea.' Aunt Mildred unstrapped her shoes.

Uncle Sal eyed her warily. 'Better leave it to me. You'll rip your pretty stockings when you catch them on the ruby.'

'That's very thoughtful. But there must be something I can do.'

'Take a mirror and search the floor in the other rooms of the suite.'

Her eyes widened. 'But one of them is Tommy's.'

'You can wait for his return if you worry about his privacy.'

Tommy trod from one foot to another until the lunch guests had made their way to the dining room. He wrinkled his nose as he inspected his natty white trousers. 'These are my best flannels,' he said. 'Aunt Mildred will be livid if I wreck them.'

'Don't tell me you have only this one pair,' Jack said.

Tommy had a sheepish look on his face as he admitted, 'The deuce is, something always happens when I wear light colours. Either I spill tomato soup or I'm directly in the way if soot from the funnels finds its way inside.' He sighed. 'Or I crawl behind a staircase where I'll lay you any odds, I'll kneel in something unsavoury.'

'Then why wear white flannels?' Frances asked.

Tommy gaped. 'Because it's the correct summer attire until we cross the equator.'

Frances giggled. 'I see. In this case, I'll take care of it.'

Before he or Jack could say another word, she squeezed herself into Tink's playground behind the staircase, and felt around with her fingertips. It was surprisingly clean, with only a few dust mites swirling in the air, as far as she could see in the half-darkness.

The day light from the glass tubes only covered a portion of the space she found herself in. At least it was roomier than she'd thought.

'Nothing here,' she said.

Jack held out his hand to help her wiggled out of it again.

'I say, there is a bit of a smear on your lovely frock. Now

I feel like a cad, letting you climb into that spot,' Tommy said.

Frances groaned inwardly. She'd purchased the dress in the second hand shop most of her wardrobe came from. So much for her hopes the tiny stain that had caused the original owner of the dress to unload it as barely worn would be unnoticeable.

'If we get a move on, we can catch today's laundry collection.' Tommy hurried towards the suite.

'The laundry?' A thought stirred.

'It usually is picked up when we're at lunch,' Tommy said. 'I hope we're still in time for our nose-bag.'

Frances broke into a trot. Jack quickened his stride.

'I'm an ass,' Tommy said, finally catching up. 'I should've let you have your lunch before dragging you here, and then bowing out of my job, to top it off.'

'It's not that. Didn't you tell me, Tink loves to play in the laundry basket?'

'Strewth.' Tommy shot towards the suite.

He barrelled through the door just as a teenaged cabin boy entered the bathroom of the suite. 'Stop,' he shouted.

The boy spun around.

'What on earth are you doing?' Aunt Mildred lifted her pince-nez and stared at him.

'You haven't found it either.' Uncle Sal's shoulders sagged.

'It's okay,' Jack said to the cabin boy. 'If you could give us five minutes?'

The cabin boy clicked his heels and obeyed.

'Tink likes the laundry basket,' Tommy said.

Aunt Mildred gave him a disappointed stare. 'You're not

supposed to let him in there. Remember when his little leg got stuck in a button-hole? He could have hurt himself.'

'I know, and I tried, but he's having so much fun.'

'Could you have a geek through the basket?' Frances asked. 'Or I could do it.'

'No,' both Aunt Mildred and Tommy said in unison.

'I'll do it.' Aunt Mildred swept into the bathroom.

'There's something I'd like to know,' Jack said.

'Sure.' Tommy leant against the table, wiping his white jacket on the spilt powder before Frances could stop him.

'Careful,' she said and pointed at the powder.

'Hand me that jacket.' Uncle Sal held out his hand. 'I've got a few tricks up my sleeve.'

Tommy groaned as he took of the garment. 'I do that all the time. But you were asking, Jack?'

'If I remember my Peter Pan, Tinkerbell's a girl fairy. Or who's Tink named for?'

'Two reasons. First of all, he was a present from my late uncle, who'd been promised it was a girl dog. He either forgot to check or it's because he was blind as a bat.'

'Nonsense.' Aunt Mildred's voice boomed. 'My husband had full use of his faculties. Corgis, as my nephew would know if he'd read anything but car magazines and racing programmes, were used as mounts by the fairies. It's a charming myth, and the reason my husband chose a corgi as my companion when the doctors told him his time was measured.'

She flounced out of the bathroom, with one hand closed around something.

'You found it,' Uncle Sal said.

She opened her hand. On her palm lay the missing

ruby. It glittered brightly in the lamplight. No wonder everyone had taken it for the real thing, Frances thought.

'Now we shall free the poor steward,' Aunt Mildred said.

Tommy's stomach rumbled. Frances felt a few hunger pangs too. Breakfast had been long ago, and since then she'd rehearsed and solved a mystery. Still, saving the steward was more important.

'Lunch first?' Tommy suggested. 'I'm sure the captain will be much more amenable once he's been fed and watered too.'

'Capital idea,' Uncle Sal said. Aunt Mildred and her vocabulary must be rubbing off, Frances thought. She was sure, an "old thing" had been on the tip of his tongue.

'One more suggestion,' Jack said. 'I'd let people know Tink doesn't carry a fortune around his neck. You don't want to tempt anyone.'

Aunt Mildred paled. 'My goodness. Why did I never think of that?'

∼

Frances wished she could have eavesdropped on the conversation between Aunt Mildred and the captain. The lady had insisted on having Major Forsythe, the burly man, who'd levelled the first accusation against the steward, come along too.

Aunt Mildred had originally intended for Frances and Jack to accompany her as well, because she credited them with solving the mystery. Jack had convinced her otherwise, and Frances agreed. The last thing they wanted was for other people to come to them with their problems. They deserved a nice uneventful voyage.

Whatever transpired, Major Forsythe returned with his face purple with suppressed rage, while Aunt Mildred smiled serenely.

Captain Grey made an appearance too. He reminded Frances of an older version of Jack, a man who didn't have to throw his weight around to make his importance felt. His entrance made the passengers in the dining room fall silent, apart from a few mutterers.

Captain Grey stood still for an instant. His arms were folded behind his back. His First Officer stood by his side. He looked so much like Gary Cooper with his blonde hair and piercing blue eyes, that Frances had to pinch herself as he whispered a few words into the captain's ears.

The stewards lined up at the far wall, in a well-rehearsed ballet.

'Most of you will know me,' Captain Grey said. 'Normally, I would have welcomed our new arrivals later today, and then handed you over to my First Officer, Mr Whalan, for your safety drill. Instead, it has come to my attention, that one of my crew was accused of theft.'

'That's right. Bloody criminal,' a man at the back of the room said.

The captain glared at the man. 'I should have said, falsely accused. The owner of the missing item has found the fake ruby, and no suspicion at all can rest on the steward who so unjustly found himself slandered.'

'Fake?' a woman's voice shrieked, as if that was worse than being wrongly accused.

'Costume jewellery. In any case, I'd like to remind you

to avail yourself of the security our ship's safe offers you for your precious belongings.' The captain scanned them all, moving his head so slowly Frances felt uncomfortable for no reason at all. 'While my crew is without exception absolutely trustworthy, the same cannot be said for everyone else. Bear that in mind, especially when you go ashore in Bombay. Bad folks will always lie in wait for unsuspecting visitors.'

'But that's weeks. You don't expect us to give up our jewels until then.' Rosalie's protest made Frances swivel her head. She was beautiful, Frances decided, if you cared for a porcelain doll with eyes as hard as marbles. In twenty years, she'd be the spitting image of her mother.

'That decision is entirely up to you,' Captain Grey said. 'But if any of you has any accusations to make, I'd ask you to come to Mr Whalan or me first instead of slandering innocent people.'

'You're sure the steward didn't pull a fast one?' Mr Callaghan and Mr Sanders snickered. Judging by their glassy eyes, they'd already visited the cocktail bar where Frances had met them only yesterday.

Captain Grey shot them a disdainful glance that quieted them. 'I will not credit that absurd notion.' He motioned Mr Whalan to follow him. 'Ladies and gentlemen, please enjoy the rest of your lunch. We will see you later.'

Frances craned her neck to see if Merry was back in the ranks of the stewards, but she couldn't spot him.

'Everything's alright now, isn't it?' she asked Jack.

'I hope so,' he said. 'Mud tends to stick, even if you started out squeaky clean.'

'No one can say a word against your mate, not with the captain backing him up,' Uncle Sal said.

Jack gave him a wry grimace and shrugged.

'I wonder why the major made such a fuss, without any proof.' Uncle Sal wrinkled his nose.

'He doesn't like Merry overmuch,' Jack said. 'He prevented Forsythe from sneaking into the pantry.'

'But there's always food,' Frances said in bewilderment. 'All he'd have to do is ask for it.'

'I also had the impression there's more to that animosity than Merry lets on. Anyway, Forsythe must have thought it a godsend to blacken his character.'

CHAPTER SEVEN

Merry reappeared before the cocktail hour. Frances and Jack had joined the queue for deck shuffleboard. Only Mr Callaghan and Mr Brown were in front of them, and both struggled to push the weighted disks with their cue-sticks anywhere near the marked scoring zones ahead of them. Luckily, the playing area was surrounded by a ten-inch high barrier, or passers-by might have been struck due to the gentlemen's spectacular bad aim.

'Don't fall for their little ploy,' Jack told Frances. 'This isn't yet a real match, but I'm sure a lot of players will underestimate these jokers after this performance.'

'Maybe they are too tipsy to play.'

'No. They pretend to be a bit top-heavy but remember these are public school boys. They may not have too much in the upper storey, but they know everything about cricket and croquet and games like shuffleboard. It's part of their upbringing.'

'Isn't that cheating, making out you're a lousy player

when you're actually bonzer?' She thought back to her novels. 'I thought that's bad form.'

He tapped her nose with a finger. 'It is. Which is why you and I, my love, will not resort to such tricks.'

Mr Callaghan and Mr Brown put away their cue-sticks and draped themselves into deck chairs, calling for a steward.

Merry shimmered into being.

'If that ain't the prodigal son.' Mr Callaghan winked at him. 'Now we've been told it's safe to be around you, please bring us two Gin Rickey. And make it quick. We're parched.'

A muscle in Merry's jaw twitched. 'Certainly, sir.'

'What a beast,' Frances said to Jack who'd watched the scene with interest. 'How dare he treat Merry like that.'

'He's used to it. Money talks, and in certain cases it's bad language.'

Jack aimed and pushed his disk onto a ten. He leant on the cue-stick. 'This is going to be good. Our cove here will soon enough get his wings clipped if I'm not mistaken.'

Indeed, Aunt Mildred made her way towards the deck chairs. Tommy followed her with two cue-sticks in one hand and Tink's leash in the other. Aunt Mildred took one of the cue-sticks and poked Mr Callaghan with it.

'Stop that,' he protested.

She poked him again, sharper. 'Don't you want to offer your chair to a lady?'

He pointed at the empty chairs around him. 'The old bird's cuckoo,' he whispered to his friend who hastened to jump up as the cue-stick came closer.

'Excuse me?' Aunt Mildred swung her improvised

weapon and hit Mr Callaghan on the shin. He half fell off the deck chair.

Merry returned on silent feet with the cocktails.

'And now I want you to apologise to this gentleman,' she said. 'And don't forget to tip him.'

Mr Callaghan and Mr Brown exchanged an embarrassed look.

'No offence meant, old boy,' Mr Callaghan mumbled as he took his drink.

'Louder, please. My hearing isn't what it used to be.' Aunt Mildred bared her teeth in a scary smile.

Laughter rose in Frances's throat. She masked it with a cough, as Mr Callaghan rose from the chair and said to the steward, 'Frightfully bad form of me. Please accept my apologies.' A bank note crinkled in his hand.

'Think no more of it.' Merry inclined his head in a way that again reminded Frances of Mr Wodehouse's inimitable Jeeves. This was better than a stage-play at the Tivoli theatre.

Aunt Mildred relaxed. 'Now I'm ready to play, Tommy, dear.'

He gave the dog a helpless look.

'We can take Tinkerbell,' Jack said.

'Would you really?'

'Sure.' Frances scooped up the little dog. He was surprisingly heavy but also adorable, with his round eyes and the wagging tail-nub.

'A negroni for me in half an hour, Merriweather,' Aunt Mildred said. She addressed Frances. 'I hope you two and Mr Bernardo will join us then for a cocktail.'

Frances changed for dinner with a mixture of excitement and regret. Her limited wardrobe would only allow for so much. She hadn't thought she'd mingle with the high and mighty on this trip.

She stuck out her tongue to her own image in the mirror. There were two choices. Either her fellow passengers accepted her as she was, or they didn't. In which case they were no loss to her.

She brushed a loose hair off her dress. If anyone wanted to look down on Frances Palmer, they were welcome to. She had Jack and Uncle Sal, and that was a lot more riches than some of the toffs could dream of.

'You look a picture.' Uncle Sal kissed her hand, every inch the gentleman in his dinner jacket. She gratefully squeezed his arm.

They knocked on Jack's door. He was the only one whose working wardrobe was up to snuff for this. Uncle Sal's evening dress dated back to his stage days and faint stains of grease paint had marked it, but it didn't matter. The only garments bought for this trip were snowy-white spats, which hid the slight lumpiness of his gammy ankle.

His bow tie sat askew. Frances righted it for him.

Jack came out of his cabin, together with Merry, who gave him a small salute before he hurried back to his duties.

'Sorry to keep you waiting,' he said. He offered Frances his arm. 'I only had to go through a few things again. The captain was originally tempted to let our pickpocket off the hook when it appeared as if Merry was as bent as a corkscrew. It would have been one thief's word against another one's.'

'But you caught the crook red-handed,' Uncle Sal said.

'Which is why he's still under lock and key.' Jack tugged at his collar. 'Shall we go and outshine the company?'

How easy it was to get used to the good life. The splendour of the dining-room still delighted Frances, but it no longer awed her. As for the company, Jack was right. Being richer didn't make them better.

Aunt Mildred, fashionable in crimson silk and matching ruby earrings, and a tuxedo-clad Tommy again shared their table. Tink's bowl already waited for the dog on his own chair.

Uncle Sal bent over Aunt Mildred's hand. 'You're a sight for sore eyes,' he said.

'You flatter me.'

'Not in the least.'

Merriweather, his features blank, weaved his way through the tables. The curious glances must have burnt a hole in his back, Frances thought, but he held his head high.

'Captain Grey begs for your company at his table, madam,' he said to Aunt Mildred.

Pink washed over her throat. Frances had judged her to be unflappable, but obviously she wasn't.

'Thank you, Merriweather. All of us?'

'Only you and Mr Clifton.'

'What about my little Tinkerbell? He always dines with me.'

'He's welcome to keep us company,' Jack said. 'He's good to have around.'

'In this case, I'm happy to accept.' She clasped her evening purse and allowed Merry and Tommy to lead her in triumph to the captain's table. Two more couples already sat there. The women dripped in jewellery and the men had the deep etched worry-lines Frances had come to recognise as the signs of too much wealth and too little control over it.

'These must be the big bananas,' Uncle Sal said. 'See that pinched look on Mr Whalan's face?'

Frances glanced around under lowered lashes. Sure enough, the First Officer tried to hide his discomfort as the simpering lady on his left inched closer and closer to him, while her husband concentrated on his oysters.

'He's working hard to earn his keep,' Jack agreed.

A dress rustled behind Frances as Evie and her friends slipped past, to be partnered by three of the bright young things, dressed in the latest fashion. Only Mr Callaghan appeared to be missing.

The men behaved better than Frances had come to expect from them. They laughed a little too loud, talked a little too much, but their companions seemed relaxed enough. Only Evie's shoulders were a little too rigid, and her smile was too bright.

The poor girl sat right within earshot of Lawrence and Rosalie as well, which must be embarrassing if she really used to be sweet on that man.

Frances couldn't see anything special in him. He had an agreeable face and nice manners but compared to Jack he paled into insignificance.

Ada's gaze flickered around until she found her original admirer a few tables away, engrossed in a chat with an elderly gentleman. A pout disappeared as fast as it had appeared.

Frances counted herself lucky that she at least had the luxury to decide whose company she kept. She raised her glass to Jack, and to Uncle Sal. 'To us.'

Tink snuffled as if in agreement. She stroked his head.

~

The ceiling fans whirred in the crowded ball room. Chandeliers lit up the stained-glass ceiling, and Frances twirled in Jack's arms. If she could bottle moments of happiness and store them forever, this would be one of them.

Uncle Sal and Aunt Mildred danced, too. Tink had been sent to the cabin, and Tommy stood chatting with Mr Fitch and Mr Sanders. Mr Brown danced with Rosalie's mother, while Frances's new friends were taken by yesterday's partners.

Already, Frances recognised faces. By the time they reached London, she would remember them all.

Her face felt hot and sweaty.

'I'll be back in a jiffy,' she said to Jack as their foxtrot ended.

'Meet me at the bar?'

She nodded and made her way to the powder room. Like the rest of the ship she'd seen so far, it could have belonged in a palace. Shell-shaped chairs in soft pink echoed the mirror frames and the wash basins set in marble.

'I'm melting.' Nancy pushed through the door as

Frances powdered her nose. The compact with Yardley's English Lavender had been a gift from Jack, and it smelt heavenly.

Nancy snapped open her jet and mother-of-pearl inlaid vanity case.

Frances had heard of them, but never seen one before. It was divided into neat compartments for powder, rouge, lipstick and eyeshadow.

'Happy?' Nancy asked.

'It's bonzer. Except I'm nervous about our performance.'

'Don't be. It'll be swell.' Nancy patted her face with a tiny powder pouffe.

The scent matched her perfume. Frances sniffed discreetly.

'You want my advice? Imagine them all as paid actors and show as much leg as possible. You'll have all the men on your side anyway, with your looks.' Nancy fluffed her hair. 'There's a few cows among the women, but they're not too bad. Mostly worried about their menfolk.' She smoothed her stockings. 'I'd better fly, or my beau will think I've abandoned him.'

'Which of them?'

Nancy grimaced. 'Old father time, I'm afraid. Although they're usually the best. Too old and well-fed to get fresh, and generous with a present or two if you're the tiniest bit nice to them.' She dangled her vanity case. 'Like this one. It came all the way from Paris.'

'Have you been there?' Frances's pulse quickened by the very idea.

'Heavens, no. I'm not that nice to my admirers. It's sold

in one of the shops on board.' She waved her fingers at Frances. 'Cheerio.'

Jack waited at the bar, with a Mimosa for Frances and a Sidecar for himself.

Uncle Sal was still dancing with Aunt Mildred and loving it. She only hoped his ankle wouldn't act up in the morning.

'You're frowning,' Jack said as he clinked glasses. 'I told you to leave your worries ashore.'

'You're right,' she said. 'I'm still pinching myself that I'm really here with you. But don't you wonder at least a tiny bit what is so important your mum asked you to drop everything?'

'It can't be life-threatening, considering how long it takes us to reach London. Otherwise she's have told me to hop on a plane.'

Frances gulped. Small aerodromes had sprung up all over Australia, and they were well-used in a country as far-flung as theirs. But flying was also risky. She remembered the international outpouring of grief when the explorer Roald Amundsen and his crew died in a crash during a rescue mission. And when the American football coach Knute Rockne had died after his plane lost a wing only this year, she'd seen grown men cry.

At least the *Empress of the Sea* possessed lifeboats and life vests. 'Didn't the captain mention a safety drill?'

'Tomorrow, before lunch. I asked young Sam, our cabin steward.'

He lifted a hand to let Uncle Sal know where they were.

Frances' godfather wiped his hot brow as he and Aunt

Mildred joined them. 'What are you having?' he asked Frances.

'A mimosa. That's champagne and orange juice.'

'One of those for me as well,' he told the bartender. 'And for my lovely friend here a Negroni.'

'Where's your nephew?' Jack asked in an abrupt manner that made both Frances and Uncle Sal raise their eyebrows.

'He was only a few minutes ago dancing with Doreen Halsall.' Aunt Mildred craned her neck and motioned towards Rosalie's mother who swooned in the arms of a slender man with brilliantined hair and a constant smile. 'Strange. There she is now, dancing with one of the professionals. I hope he can improve her sense of rhythm. That woman has no rhythm.'

Jack put his drink down. 'If you'll excuse me,' Jack said.

'What's wrong?' Frances asked.

'I saw our old friend Callaghan buzzing around as if he's searching for someone, and I'm afraid that one might be Tommy.'

'Callaghan? Oh, I see.' Aunt Mildred pushed her drink aside. 'Let's go.'

'You ladies stay here,' Jack said. 'If there's trouble, having an audience will make it worse.'

Uncle Sal staid his lady-friend with one hand. 'Our Jack's right.'

'Any idea where Tommy would go?'

'He's fond of star-gazing.' Aunt Mildred's lips nearly disappeared in a grim line. 'There are enough dark corners on the observation deck to do heaven only knows what.'

CHAPTER EIGHT

*J*ack strolled to the door, a carefree grin on his face. As soon as he'd reached the passage, he broke into a trot. A flight of stairs took him to the middle of the deck. He stood still, until his vision adjusted from the bright lights to the semi-darkness around him.

The games area was still busy although all the equipment had been locked away for the night. Nevertheless, a middle-aged group of men practiced their swings with imaginary cue-sticks.

Jack turned left. Smooching noises and giggles told him he wouldn't find his target here either.

He moved close to the inside wall, passing a steward. 'This area will be closed at midnight, sir,' he said.

That gave Jack half an hour for his search. He found Callaghan and Tommy squaring off the each other at the farthest end.

Callaghan had raised his fists in the correct boxer's

stance. Tommy stood with his back against the wall, already at a disadvantage, but undaunted.

'What's going on, gentlemen?'

Jack's voice startled Callaghan. He spun around. 'None of your business, old chap.'

'I wouldn't be so sure of that.' Jack smiled, a relaxed, friendly smile that tended to disarm his men. 'Again, what's the problem here?'

'This gentleman here has taken umbrage with my aunt,' Tommy said.

'The old bird embarrassed me in front of my friend.'

Jack sighed. 'The thing is, mate, you did the embarrassing yourself.' He clapped a hand on Callaghan's shoulder and squeezed.

The young man yelped as Jack hit a nerve.

'Wouldn't it be much nicer if you apologised and we could all be friends? I'm sure you didn't intend to be rude, and if you tell Mrs Clifton as much, she'll shake your hand, and all will be forgotten.'

He sniffed Callaghan's breath. 'A word to the wise, stick to one poison. Gin on top of rum and whisky is a sure way to ruin.'

He released Callaghan from his grip and clapped him on the back.

Callaghan wavered.

'Take it from someone a lot older than you,' Jack lied. Despite his juvenile behaviour, the little louse must be close to thirty. The first lines already showed around his bloodshot eyes, and they were not caused by the sun. Red veins on his nose pointed at heavy boozing.

Mr Brown came upon the scene. 'Here you are, Callaghan. We're all waiting in the smoking room.'

He peered at Jack and Tommy. 'Am I interrupting something?'

Callaghan hesitated.

Jack wiggled his fingers, a move he'd found to be much more intimidating than a loud knuckle cracking.

'Everything's just dandy,' Callaghan said. 'Come on. I have a few hands to win.'

Mr Brown let out a deep breath. 'You always have a fiendish luck.'

Jack took him to be the younger and more intelligent one of the two. He'd soon grow out of his admiration for the loutish Callaghan, if it even existed.

He nudged Tommy who held out a hand. 'No hard feelings?'

Callaghan had no choice but to accept the peace offer. 'None whatsoever,' he said. 'Care to join us for a game?'

Tommy shuffled.

'That'd be smashing,' Jack answered for him.

The steward stepped aside for them. Jack gave him a hasty message for Frances and Aunt Mildred. The game could be interesting, he thought. There was no better way to discover a man's characters than to see him handle victories and defeat. Or to plumb the depth of his honesty.

As they entered the gambling salon, Jack wished he had his sketch book with him. The scene in front of him appealed to all his artistic senses. The colour scheme was muted, with brown leather furniture, walnut wall panelling, and bronze lamp fittings. White shirt fronts blazed in the light as men sat together to smoke cigars, chat, or play at one of the five card tables.

Tobacco smoke curled in the air. The club owner in Jack applauded the shrewdness of the designer. The room looked masculine enough to make it unnecessary to forbid women entrance. It was also easy to clean in the early hours, despite the lack of outside windows to let in fresh air. As magnificent as a black and white or black and gold interior would have been, pipe and tobacco ash would have ruined its appearance in no time flat.

'Are you playing?' Callaghan reached for a deck of cards. His eyes sparkled in anticipation. 'Baccarat.'

'You're the dealer?' There were no mirrors in the room, a fact that would make it harder for card sharps to ply their trade.

'We take turns.'

Tommy took out his wallet and handed over a tenner in return for a stack of chips.

An hour passed amenable enough in which Jack studied his new buddies. He could easily have cleaned up, thanks to his skill at counting cards he'd honed on his job. To flush out any cheats, he had to know all the tricks.

Tommy was a decent player, who erred on the side of caution.

Callaghan tended to be overly aggressive and hell-bent on making up for any loss with big raises and high risks. His slight inebriation didn't help.

Brown played an old-fashioned game. No big gambles, but also no ill humour when he lost.

Fitch and Sanders seemed to base their decisions on a

non-existent strategy, so their wins were more flukes than anything else.

Under his lashes, Jack studied the other tables. On one, a craps game attracted a lot of attention. More often than not, Major Forsythe, the man who had been so fast to throw accusations at Merry, won. The stack of chips next to him must be worth at least twenty quid.

Lawrence Vaughan played at his table, too, with considerably less luck. Any professional gambler worth his salt would have considered him as the perfect mark, with his lack of attention and disregard of odds.

'Stop day-dreaming,' one of the other players urged him. 'If it's your sweetheart you're mooning about, she's not here.'

Lawrence shoved a stack of chips into the centre. 'Very funny.' He called a four as he rolled the dice.

A six showed up. 'Bad luck, old boy,' Forsythe said. His own throw as more successful.

Jack made a mental note to ask Merry if the dice were supplied by the ship or if they could be replaced. It would also be interesting to discover if the craps player usually cashed in.

Although card sharps tended to prefer short trips, where they could get off board before their victims suspected anything but a bout of bad luck, Jack intended to keep his eyes open. He'd seen his fair share of weighted dice and marked cards.

Tommy yawned.

'Last game for me, gentlemen,' Jack said. He peeked at his two cards. A ten and an eight. Fitch, whose turn it was to be the dealer, had a nine.

Jack signalled he was done. Tommy did the same.

Callaghan bought another card, a queen. He swore and threw down his hand. Sanders accepted a third card and allowed himself a tiny smirk that would bankrupt him at poker. Brown was done, too.

They revealed their hands. The bank had nineteen. Jack, Sanders and Brown admitted defeat. Tommy turned his cards around. An ace and a nine. That brought his winnings of the night to two pound and four, only three shillings less than Jack.

He accompanied Tommy to his suite and was promptly invited to come in for a nightcap. Jack was about to decline when he realised this would be a good occasion to learn more about his fellow travellers. There were a few things that bothered him, and Tommy had shown himself to be a lot more intelligent than he'd seemed at first sight.

~

In the bar, Aunt Mildred watched with trepidation as Jack left. 'I do hope Tommy's not in trouble,' she said. 'He's supposed to be a decent boxer, at least he was at Cambridge, but I'm not sure Mr Callaghan would follow the Marquess of Queensberry rules.'

'You don't have to worry while Captain Jack's around,' Uncle Sal said.

'Captain Jack?'

'He shipped out in 1914,' Frances said. 'Most of his staff served with him.'

'Loyalty. The first sign of a gentleman.' Aunt Mildred sipped her Negroni.

'Have you had a run-in with Callaghan before?'

'No, and we've travelled together on our way to Australia, too. He and his friends joined the ship in Bombay. I understood their families are in the plantation business.'

'And the men themselves?' Uncle Sal asked.

'Busy being bright young things. If any of them has ever done an honest day's work, I'll be surprised.' A faint sneer flitted over her face. 'My nephew might appear a bit foppish, but I assure you, I wouldn't let him sit around idle.'

'What is it that he does?' Frances couldn't help but wonder how working for one's living and travelling for months with one's aunt could be combined.

'He used to be my late husband's secretary and once we're back in London, he'll take up a position in the Foreign Office. Lowly, but respectable.'

A thrill shot through Frances. The Foreign Office sounded frightfully posh and exciting. She'd underestimated Tommy.

'Is that why Mr Callaghan doesn't like him? It can't be because you showed him up when he was so nasty to Merriweather.'

'I have no idea. It's not really the kind of behaviour a gentleman would indulge in.'

'It seemed to me the young fool thought the steward really was guilty of something,' Uncle Sal said.

'Ridiculous. Even if that man were possessed of two brain cells to rub together, he wouldn't have any reason to call out Tommy over it.' Aunt Mildred's brow furrowed. 'Unless somebody egged him on.'

'Somebody who dislikes Tommy? Or is it still about Merriweather?'

'What possible case can one have to hold a grudge against a mere steward?'

Frances thought back to the pickpocket, but she'd promised to keep quiet about that incident, and anyway it had nothing to do with Callaghan's odious behaviour.

'They've been gone an awful long time,' Frances said. She was used to Jack sweeping in, and in a flash, any sticky situation would be resolved.

A steward glided in, surveying the bar guests before heading towards her. They really moved differently from other people, Frances thought in a bewildered moment, before her brain could register fear for Jack and Tommy.

'Is everything alright?' Her voice rose. Uncle Sal squeezed her hand.

'Mr Sullivan asked me to tell you he and Mr Clifton would be in the smoking-room with the other gentleman, and that he wishes you not to wait up.'

'I see. Thank you.'

Aunt Mildred harrumphed. 'Gambling, no doubt. Doreen told me her daughter's fiancé is usually in for a bloodletting.'

Frances detected a hint of disapproval. 'Jack's no gambler,' she said. 'He will have a good reason to go along.'

'I hope so. Not that Tommy has shown any signs of developing a taste for gambling, but you never know.' Aunt Mildred hid a yawn.

'Don't worry,' Uncle Sal said. 'I'd trust Jack Sullivan and his good sense with my life. Will we see you for breakfast?'

'Thanks for coming to the rescue,' Tommy said as he poured them two snifters of brandy. 'Not that I can't hold my own, but it's devilish awkward to have a fistfight on the deck. Turning up with a black eye or sending Callaghan to be stitched up wouldn't be the thing either.'

'Does he easily get riled?' Jack asked.

Tommy shrugged. 'He used to be easy-going until lately. At first I thought he wanted to impress one of the girls his friends dangle after.'

'Girls?'

'The dancers. He tried his luck with the pretty red-head, but that was more to annoy Larry.'

Jack gave him a questioning look.

'Lawrence Vaughan. Engaged to the fair Rosalie, but when he had an eye-full of Evie Miles, his future mother-in-law couldn't call him to order fast enough. Mind you, it was only a mild flirtation, if at all. He's not the type to step out of line.'

'You seem to know a lot about these people.'

'It's not that hard when people think you're the brainless sort. And Aunt Mildred and Doreen Halsall have moved in the same circles for years.'

'I got the impression there was not a lot of love lost between them.'

'There isn't. Doreen and her daughter have made their way into society thanks to old Halsall's business skills.'

'I didn't take your aunt to be such a snob.'

'You got the wrong end of the stick. It's Mrs Halsall who tries to hide their humble beginnings.'

Jack swilled his brandy. 'From all I've seen, I can't blame her.'

'It is a bit silly, when I think of it. Still, it's how it's always been. Another snifter?'

'Another day. I'll leave you to your beauty sleep.'

The ship lay in silence as he made his way along the dim passage to his cabin. The thick carpet and the heavy metal doors swallowed any sound from outside, or the decks above. The Top Note would be closed by now, and all of Adelaide should be fast asleep.

In his cabin, he switched on his bedside lamp and took up his pencil. Without thinking about it, in a few swift strokes he sketched someone he hadn't thought about in years, an old man with a bent back and arthritic hands, still in his servant's uniform despite his seventy-odd years.

That was a memory from the last time Jack had seen his grandfather, when he spent a precious leave from the front in London, in the spring of 1918. Old Jonathan Sullivan was a staunch defender of the Empire, the feudalism, and the idea of keeping to one's station in life. He'd died ten years ago, penniless but for the small stipend his former daughter-in-law convinced him to accept once in a blue moon. His feckless son, Jack's dad, had long ago disappeared somewhere in Australia.

Old Jonathan; proud, poor and too obstinate to think twice about necessary changes in the world. He wondered what his grandfather would have made of this new world, and of Jack himself.

CHAPTER NINE

The steward's knock roused Frances. Eight o'clock! She jumped out of her bed and banged her shin on the chair she'd pulled up the night before, to use as a clothes horse.

She rubbed the sore spot. A bruise might shine through her stockings when she stood in the spotlight. She'd have to ask Uncle Sal what to do if her shin turned purple.

A bit of cold water splashed into her face helped her wake up completely. She brushed her teeth with one hand and her hair with the other, desperate not to miss Jack before she and Uncle Sal had to rehearse.

She was lucky. He already sat at their table, chatting with Uncle Sal. Both men were bright-eyed and brimming with energy, but then they were used to late nights.

Aunt Mildred and Tommy hadn't appeared yet. Neither had any of their other acquaintances, so they could at least talk freely.

To be safe from any earwigging, Frances nevertheless lowered her voice. 'How did it go last night?'

A steward sat a plate with eggs and toast in front of her. 'I've ordered you Billy tea again,' Jack said as he buttered his toast.

'I hope they didn't take it from Evie's supply.'

'Aunt Mildred made them search through their pantry yesterday until they unearthed some.' Uncle Sal chortled. 'She told them it was their patriotic duty to reflect all commonwealth countries they called on in the kitchen, and kedgeree and devilled kidneys weren't enough.'

A steaming pot with Billy tea proved him right.

'You didn't answer my question,' Frances said two minutes later. The distraction had almost succeeded.

'There's not much to tell. Callaghan had dipped into his cup a bit too heavily and decided to work off his sense of injured pride. A few calm words, and he saw sense. We all parted as friends after a spot of cards.'

'Everything above board?' Uncle Sal tapped his nose.

'I think so. Although the major who was so convinced of Merry's guilt had the devil's own luck.'

'At least he calls himself major,' Uncle Sal said. 'I heard him chat with Callaghan while you were dancing. One of those fire-eaters, used to ordering around a bunch of native servants. Pukka sahib and all that stuff.'

'Honorary title? He didn't strike me as a military man.'

Jack's judgement of people tended to be reliable. 'You don't like him,' Frances said.

'I don't like anyone who believes they're superior only because they were born with a silver spoon in their mouth, or at least pretend to.' He laid his hand on Frances's. 'I'm afraid that kind of thinking is a good preparation for merry old England.'

He left Frances and Uncle Sal to prepare for their big show. The observation deck wasn't open yet, but the proper deck was. Petrels dived in and out of the water far below him, and seals bobbed on the waves.

Jack breathed in the salty air. Only two other passengers braved the open space and its keen breeze that ruffled their hair.

He leant on the railing. Everything around him was different shades of blue, silver, pink and gold, like an exquisite water colour.

He pulled his rolled-up sketch book out of his pocket. Tomorrow he'd bring his treasured Leica, to take photographs.

He studied the movement of the birds. Their long stiff wings and tube-nosed-bill made them a joy to sketch. When he finally stopped, he had a crick in his neck and found two hours to have passed. If he wanted to snap pictures of Frances and Uncle Sal during their rehearsal, he'd have to hurry.

He caught them at the tail-end of their session. He'd hidden himself away behind a curtain, as not to disturb them. They were practicing their magic act now, a late addition to their performance. Frances's mouth formed an o in pretend excitement as she pulled a long row of knotted handkerchiefs out of Uncle Sal's pocket.

He pressed the button of his Leica and hoped the lighting was good enough to do without a flash bulb.

'What are you doing there?'

Jack spun around, to find a pretty girl glaring daggers at

him. Then her stance softened, as she recognised him. 'You're the fiancé,' she said. 'I thought you were spying on Frances.'

'Are you rehearsing too?'

'A new dance, for the costume ball at the end of our first week at sea.' She rolled her eyes. 'Or rather, an old one. Nancy, Ada and me are supposed to do a tame version of Josephine Baker's Banana Dance. Unless we can come up with a better idea, we're stuck with it.'

The Banana Dance! Jack remembered the furore and scandal caused by the skimpy costume, and the moves, and that had been during the height of the Roaring Twenties, in scandal used Paris. 'I'd have thought it a little risqué,' he said diplomatically.

'That's what I've been trying to tell the Second Officer. He's in charge of entertainment and found an old magazine with Josephine on the cover in the library.' Her lip wobbled. 'It's hard enough to make people treat us with respect. Flouncing around on stage in banana skirts is not doing us any favours.'

'Good grief.' An image of the Second Officer, stolid, fortyish Mr Mackie, popped into his mind, just before the man himself came into view.

Frances and Uncle Sal left the stage, glowing with satisfaction. 'That should do until tomorrow night,' he said to them before they disappeared behind a bamboo screen where they hid their props.

Jack lingered.

'Where are your friends?' Mr Mackie ignored Jack as he addressed Evie.

'My colleagues will be here any second, sir.'

Jack tapped him in the shoulder. 'Could I have a word?'

Mr Mackie peered at him. 'Oh, it's you, Mr Sullivan. Don't tell me there's anything wrong with your companion's act.'

'They're good-oh. It's just – I heard there's going to be a costume ball.'

'Two, actually.' Mr Mackie preened. 'The second one is just before we reach London. It'll be Christmas themed and will be a smash hit.'

'I can't wait,' Jack said. 'I assume you'll have plenty of thrills for us in store.'

'I try, Mr Sullivan, I try. Between you and me, this young lady here and her colleagues will dazzle us with the Banana Dance.'

Jack faked a cough. 'Oh, I say.' He silently implored Evie to be quiet. 'I'm sure it would be spectacular, only ...' He shook his head.

'Only?'

'You're aware I run a nightclub? Nothing tawdry, but even those of my competitors who are a little less strict when it comes to certain customer expectations, would stay away from an act like that. The women are usually scandalised, and some of the men get the wrong idea if you catch my drift. Sorry, Miss Miles.'

Mr Mackie's permanent tan deepened. 'I didn't think of that.'

Jack pretended to think. 'What I'd do, is get the passengers involved. A nice little number, where your professional dancers and a few select ladies and gentlemen of the audience have a moment in the spotlight. Miss Miles here is an excellent singer, so maybe a duet with one of the passengers would be a good addition to the programme.'

'I see.' The Second Officer rubbed his nose. 'What do you think, Miss Miles?'

'It's a smashing idea,' she said, beaming all over her pretty face. 'We can easily work something out, together with Pierre and Sergei.'

'I'd need a list of suggestions, which passengers we should approach.'

'You'll have it tonight, sir.' Evie sashayed towards her two friends, who burst into the room.

'I'm so sorry, we're late.' Ada's head drooped in fake remorse as she spotted Mr Mackie. 'We ran into a few of the passengers, and they wouldn't let us go.'

'In a manner of speaking,' Nancy hastened to add as Mr Mackie's jaw set in a hard line. 'We didn't want to be rude. Now, where are our costumes?'

Jack slipped away, grinning to himself. The infamous Banana Dance. He'd seen it at the pictures, and he'd bet anything Mr Mackie had only heard of it.

'Did you watch?' Frances snuggled into Jack's arms as he caught up with them on the observation deck. Uncle Sal discreetly gave them space as he went in search of refreshments.

'Only the final number,' he said. 'You'll bowl them over.'

She crossed her fingers. 'I couldn't bear it if I mess things up for Uncle Sal.'

He pressed a kiss onto her forehead. 'Impossible. What shall we do after lunch? Play shuffleboard, or tennis, or watch the cricket?'

A small corridor for the game had been cordoned off,

and a large group clad in blinding white formed an orderly line, with two crew members acting as cricket team captains.

Although Australia had caught the sports fever like the rest of the Commonwealth, Frances secretly wished cricket were faster. It could take hours before the excitement set in, and that was with seasoned players.

'Would you mind if I go down to the library? Back home I hardly get around to read more than a magazine.'

She hadn't lied to him, Frances reasoned as they went their separate ways after lunch and a lifeboat drill that had at first seemed bewildering, with everyone running to and from to reach their designated assembly points. Seeing the boats for herself and their sturdiness had reassured her.

Uncle Sal declared he'd have a rest in a deckchair after their exertion, and Jack planned to play shuffleboard. She still intended to spend the afternoon reading and writing a letter to her mum that she'd post in Bombay. A tiny detour to the shops wouldn't hurt. If Jack had come along, he'd only insisted on buying her a present. Instead, she might surprise him with a gift for once.

Frances had expected there to be one or two shops midships. Instead, she might as well have been in the Adelaide Arcade. A busy beauty salon took up more space than the Palmer's house. She peeked into the shop window, with its display of hand-held mirrors, powder compacts and silver backed brushes. Three ladies had their hair styled in the back of the room, and two manicurists sat side by side next to the door. One of them polished Rosalie's nails.

Frances inspected her own hands. She kept her

fingernails blunt and short, but apart from that her hands might as well have belonged to a society lady. Her hand cream to keep them soft was one of the few luxuries Frances had allowed herself since the beginning of the Great Depression.

She strolled on. A gent's outfitters came next, with evening dress displayed on a clothes horse, next to cricket gear and knickerbockers.

A ladies' store advertised fancy dress for the costume ball. Painted silk fans in red, gold and white and oversized feather fans in white and black drew her in. She moved as close as she could to see if there were any price tags.

'Shopping?' Evie asked behind her.

Frances gave a start. 'More like dreaming about it.'

'Don't. It's all overpriced. Wait until we reach port. That's where you can lay your hands on really spectacular things for a few shillings.'

Frances spotted a cigarette case just like Evie's in the jeweller's display. Only this one had a blue stone set in the clasp. She pointed at it. 'They do have pretty stuff.'

'Very pretty, and expensive. These shops aren't exactly made for you and me.'

'I was hoping to find something nice for Jack,' Frances said.

Evie's face lit up. 'He's a swell guy. Did he tell you he saved us from having to make total fools of ourselves on stage?'

'Do you have to say yes to everything?'

'We're hired as entertainers.' Evie shrugged. 'Dance classes in the afternoon, partnering lonely men in the evening, and a show performance when desired, whatever is needed.'

'And singing.'

'That's the part of the job I love.' Evie hummed to herself, before she gave a little yelp. 'Gosh, here I am, chatting, and I'm supposed to pick up the fabric for our new costumes, now that the rubber banana skirts are to be no more.'

'How fancy is the ball going to be?' Frances gave the feather fans another longing glance. They were stunning.

'Very, but you don't have to spend any money on a costume. Come by our dressing room tomorrow before lunch and we'll sort you out.'

Rosalie and her mother left the beauty salon, with their hair in glossy curls.

Evie ducked and darted into the fabric shop, almost as if she was hiding.

∼

In the library, Frances browsed through the well-stacked bookcases. All the classic novels she'd ever heard of were here, next to modern literature. To her delight, one whole shelf was dedicated to the works of Mr Wodehouse, and another held every single of Agatha Christie's works.

Then there were Virginia Woolf, Ernest Hemingway and D.H. Lawrence, all writers she'd heard of, but never read. She almost drooled.

A slim gloved hand pulled *A Passage to India* out of the shelf next to her; Aunt Mildred.

'I hope you're not a bluestocking, or given to smut,' she said to Frances.

'I don't think so,' she replied, bewildered.

'Good. I've heard more than I ever cared about, fawning over the wild intensity and raw emotion of that Lawrence fellow or that Woolf woman. Balderdash.' She aimed her pince-nez at Frances. 'Well, have you made your choice?'

Dutifully, Frances selected *Carry On, Jeeves* and a six months old copy of *Vogue*.

Aunt Mildred patted her arm. 'Well chosen. Now you'll excuse me.'

Frances glanced around. An armchair in the corner seemed the perfect spot to read unobserved, and next to it paper and pen on a small table made it ideal for letter-writing, too. There was the official writing room, too, but this would do nicely.

She took one of the creamy sheets with the ship's letterhead and unscrewed her pen.

'Dear Mum,

So much has happened that I hardly know where to start. You should see the ball room, where Uncle Sal and I are to perform tomorrow night. It's big enough to hold eight hundred people ...'

She wrote and wrote, until she'd filled four pages and run out of things to say. If she went on at this rate, it would cost a fortune to post that letter in a bit under three weeks.

'Writing home?' Evie scanned the room and sank into a chair opposite Frances, hiding behind a copy of *Tatler*.

'Mum has never been outside Australia,' Frances said. 'She'll be dying to hear about this, so I thought I'd tell her everything that happens.'

'You should keep a diary,' Evie said. 'But if you plan on writing her a really long letter, you should use airmail. It only takes days for your letter to arrive, and it can be cheaper too.'

'I thought it would cost a fortune, with a fat letter like mine.'

'You use special paper.' Evie jumped up, only to sink back into her seat and lift the magazine again, as Lawrence Vaughan came into sight.

A faint pink washed over her face.

The young man glanced around. Evie pulled in her feet, as she was trying to make herself invisible.

'Larry,' Rosalie cooed from the door just as her fiancé headed towards Frances and Evie. He gave a start.

'Coming, darling. I'm only grabbing something to read.' He hurried back to the magazine section and helped himself to a dog-eared copy of *Fortune*.

Evie's head popped up as soon as he'd left. She went to the corner desk and opened a drawer.

'Here it is.' She put a few almost weightless blue sheets on the table. 'Your mum will get a thrill just opening this.'

As she left, Frances picked up her pen to copy everything she'd written so far. What an odd company they'd found themselves in.

~

On the observation deck, Jack shut out everything else, from the chatter of fellow passengers to the chugging from the engines, as he filled page after page of his sketch book. Most of them contained just a few charcoal lines, here a man flinging his quoits, there a woman leaning on the rail, her rigid shoulders hinting at self-control and anger, a dainty tea set on a side table.

They didn't need more details. No one else would ever see them, even if he should use one or two for a proper painting. He'd treated himself to a new set of watercolours and paper from Winsor & Newton, with a fat stack of paper from the same company. His battered easel stood ready in his cabin, hidden from view by a bamboo screen. He had until they'd dock in London in mid-December to finish his present work, a portrait of his sister Rachel intended for his mother.

Those two had last seen each other at the end of 1923. Eight years, in which his sister had battled heartbreak and nightmares, until he packed her off to their aunt and uncle in New Zealand. Now Rachel was engaged to be married to a station owner and blissfully happy. One less worry for him.

He closed his sketch book. He hadn't admitted it to Frances, but the summons from his mother had unsettled him. She usually came straight to the point, when she needed help. No shilly-shallying and hoping he'd get the message. So, what made it so important that he cross the ocean, that she couldn't tell him what was going on?

CHAPTER TEN

Frances rifled through the dancers' wardrobe. Two nights until the costume ball, so she had to decide on something.

'How about this? It's new.' Nancy held up a green, feather trimmed dress with a low-cut back and a matching mask. 'Or you could go as an Egyptian Queen. We could use a sheet to make the dress.'

'I'm going to be a Ziegfeld girl.' Ada picked a short, sequinned dress that revealed more than it covered. 'A vamp, with class.'

'Don't scare your beau away until you've got him hooked,' Nancy said.

Ada pouted at her.

'What are you wearing, Eve?' Frances asked.

'She always goes as a mermaid, all frothy tulle and sparkling green and blue sequins.' Ada tapped on the wall clock. 'Make up your mind, girls. We have a dance class coming up.'

'And I bet you pass on all the cornshredders to me.'

Nancy pouted. 'How can you tell which ones are going to tread on your toes like clockwork?'

'They all do, darling. Otherwise they wouldn't need classes.'

'Your present admirer doesn't, and neither did Evie's Larry.'

'Can we please stop mentioning him?' Evie sounded exasperated, and sad.

They all turned to Frances. 'The green dress is perfect for you,' she said to Evie. 'You'll look like a film star in it.'

Evie stroked the soft satin. 'Are you sure? Would you like my mermaid costume instead? Or we can rig you up as an Egyptian princess.'

'I'd love that.' Frances looked at her hands. They trembled. 'Sorry to be such a bore. I wish tonight was over.'

'Stage fright?'

'A little. What if the ship cranks and I lose my balance?'

'You won't. And if you are in trouble on stage, pat your hair as a signal, and Ada will shriek and faint into someone's arms.' Nancy giggled. 'That's something worth seeing.'

Ada allowed herself a smug grin. 'My best performance. It works like a charm.'

'Why would you faint? Or don't you need a reason?' Frances asked.

'Heat and excitement. I'd have screamed there's a mouse, only then there'll be a panic, and the purser will chew us out.'

'There are no mice or rats on board, are there?' Not that Frances was afraid of rodents, although she preferred them at a safe distance.

Evie shrugged. 'If so, they'll be in the pantry, with all the food. Any rodent showing its furry face will soon enough be taken care of. So, don't forget, we're there for you if you need a distraction for the audience.'

∼

Frances stepped onto the stage, her glossy blonde wig firmly in place. She placed her hand in Uncle Sal's and curtsied as the drummer played a solo to announce them. The audience cheered.

∼

Frances willed herself not to look at them. There must be at least five hundred people watching her, but that didn't matter. What mattered was becoming Signorina Francesca, lovely assistant of Sal the Magnificent.

The room went dim, apart from the stage. Uncle Sal helped her into the ankle and wrist straps before he sat in his chair.

The drums started again, and the turntable with the chair on top moved, slowly, so slowly, until it picked up speed and Uncle Sal was spun around.

The first knife cut through the air and embedded itself between Frances's left shoulder and her neck.

The audience gasped.

The table kept on turning, relentlessly, as the second knife landed between her other shoulder and her neck.

∼

Half an hour later, their show ended with deafening applause. Uncle Sal and Frances bowed and bowed, until her legs went wobbly and they were allowed to leave the stage.

She glowed. Their act had gone off without a hitch, and she'd never seen Uncle Sal this happy since his retirement. He'd performed at the Top Note with her, but that was playing to friends, and a home crowd. These people had seen the world. They wouldn't have clapped their hands raw for a second-rate entertainer.

In the dressing room, she removed the wig and fluffed out her hair. Her nose needed powder, but first she'd need to change her dress.

Her face still felt hot. A few moments of fresh air, and then she'd join Uncle Sal and Jack in the ball room.

The night breeze cooled her off as soon as she went outside. Voices stopped her, and someone else too, because the clicking of heels behind her disappeared.

A man said, 'I feel like a cad for throwing her over like that, but I have to. It's not fair otherwise, and she deserves better.'

The voice sounded like Lawrence Vaughan's. Frances's ears burnt. She stole away as he went on. 'Even if you won't forgive me, I'll do it, right after the ball.'

Frances hastened down the staircase.

Uncle Sal held court at the bar. A half empty champagne bottle showed her they'd started the celebrations without her.

Aunt Mildred raised a glass to Frances. 'A splendid show, my dear. I felicitate you.'

Frances blushed. 'Thank you. I don't really want people to know its me.'

'Nonsense.' Aunt Mildred drained her glass. Tommy refilled it.

'You have nothing to be ashamed of. I've already complimented Sal on his choice. It's refreshing to see a pretty young thing like you on the stage, without being half-naked.'

Frances was unsure whether to be pleased or hurt. Was her beautiful costume old-fashioned?

'Don't make a face like that,' Aunt Mildred said. 'I have nothing against showing a bit of skin, within reason. Like our dance girls. Titillating, yet tasteful, although you can tell the blonde one is on the make.'

Frances glanced around. Ada and her admirer danced so close together, it would have been hard to put as much as a newspaper between them. Nancy smiled bravely as her usual partner trod on her foot. She couldn't see Evie, or Jack.

'Where is Jack?' she asked.

'He's been kind enough to take Tinkerbell for a last stroll before bedtime. I didn't want Tink to miss your show, and your fiancé thought it best if Merryweather isn't seen with my darling until this silliness is completely forgotten.'

Uncle Sal handed Frances a weak Mimosa. She preferred the champagne to be only a splash as a refreshment.

'My Tink has taken quite a shine to your Jack.'

'He loves dogs,' Frances said. 'And cats. But he's so busy with work he says it wouldn't be fair on the animal to have one.' She paused.

'And what about you? I don't trust people who don't like animals.' Aunt Mildred's gaze fixed on Doreen Halsall, who made her way into the ball room, with her vanity case in her hand.

'We used to have both when my father was alive,' Frances said. 'But these days it's hard enough to feed oneself.'

Tommy gave her a sympathetic glance. 'You're right, and with your fiancé busy with Tink, may I have this dance?'

They glided across the dance floor. He wasn't a born dancer, but definitely not a cornshredder, she decided.

'I say, you're not peeved with my aunt, are you? She's a bit blunt when she likes someone, but she means well,' he said.

'She's a bit scary, don't you think?'

'When I was young, she made me quake in my boots just peering at me through her pince-nez. But she's a good sort, and she and your Uncle Sal seem to be getting on famously.'

'Your family seems frightfully posh,' Frances said.

He raised his eyebrows in a comical manner. 'Not frightfully. One does have one's connections and a certain family history, but nothing to be intimidated by.'

'It's only – we'll probably never see you again after this voyage, but if we should run into you, would she be likely to snub Uncle Sal?' There. It was out.

Tommy made a wrong step and instantly apologised. 'Heavens, no. Much more likely that she'll claim all his time. She isn't really a snob, you know. Only picky with who she approves of.'

He glanced over her shoulder. 'There's Jack. I assume I have to hand you over now.'

～

Frances floated to her cabin, only to be brought up short by the sight of Evie walking up and down the passage.

'Is anything wrong?' she asked.

Evie hesitated for an instant. 'Nancy's had too much giggle water, and Ada was taking her back to our cabin. Only she must have forgotten about me and locked it without taking the key out of the hole.'

'Do you want to come with me?' Frances unlocked her room. 'You can either try later to rouse them, or your welcome to stay here. There's a second bed.'

'That would be wonderful, if you're sure.' Evie's pale skin was almost translucent with fatigue.

'Sure. When do you need to rise in the morning?'

CHAPTER ELEVEN

By the time the costume ball rolled around, Frances had settled into an easy routine. A leisurely breakfast, a stroll along the deck followed by shuffleboard, and then reading either in the library or in a deck chair. The evenings were spent either in the ball room, dancing, or in the piano bar where the music was a welcome background for chatting with Jack, or Tommy and his aunt, and Uncle Sal.

Her letter home hadn't increased by much. She'd been too busy not doing much for once.

She adjusted her Egyptian dress. A black and golden collar and a cuff were all she needed to become an exotic creature from another era. Evie had promised to add the winged kohl eyeliner to complete Frances's make-up.

Jack would come as a cowboy, courtesy of the ship's stores. Uncle Sal had declined to tell her in advance.

At five minutes to eight, her cavaliers stood outside her cabin. Jack looked magnificent with his gun holster and the

Stetson pulled deep into his face. 'Howdy, ma'am?' he greeted her.

Uncle Sal was harder to recognise, with his white face and triangular eyebrows. He turned his toes outwards and waddled like a penguin. 'You're Charlie Chaplin,' she cried.

He bobbed his head, obviously already in character. If he intended to keep his silence all night long, Aunt Mildred would be disappointed. She giggled as they set off.

At the staircase, they ran into Larry Vaughan and his fiancée who impersonated Harlequin and Columbine.

'Excuse me, sir?' Cabin boy Sam ran after the couple. 'You lost your key.'

Larry patted his pockets and slipped Sam a crown. 'How stupid. Thank you.'

~

The ballroom dazzled Frances. Paper garlands, tinsel and twinkling lights were strung all across the ceiling, and the orchestra was dressed up in turbans, silk shirts and baggy trousers.

'Madame de Pompadour, I presume.' Uncle Sal bowed to a lady with a powdered white wig and a crinoline dress. A turbaned servant held her ostrich fan. Frances had to look twice before she recognised Tommy and his aunt.

The show started off with a laugh. The male professional dancers started on their own, with a ballet parody. Evie, Nancy and Ada joined them, and they brought company, wearing tutus over their pants. After some confusion Frances identified Mr Brown and Mr Fitch, and one of the cigar-smoking gentlemen who usually claimed Nancy. The men tiptoed around in circles, fluttering their arms. The audience broke into riotous laughter.

Mr Mackie, now a pirate with a fake scar and an eye-patch, swaggered over to Jack who stood with Frances at the bar, ordering refreshments. 'Much better than the Banana Dance,' he said. 'I'm obliged to you.'

'My pleasure,' Jack said. 'Would you care to join us for a drink?'

Mr Mackie licked his lips. 'Maybe later. I'm on duty until ten.'

'We'll see you then.'

The dancers left the stage, and the ball began in earnest.

Evie, Ada and Nancy took a break at one of the coveted tables closest to the bar. Or maybe they were working, considering how many people stopped to congratulate them, Frances mused. The male dancers were kept on their feet. Even Doreen and Rosalie Halsall complimented the girls as they swayed past in the arms of the professionals.

'That was a most charming number,' Doreen said as her partner tipped her, and her hand fluttered graciously close to Evie and Ada's backs.

'I wish you'd convinced my darling Larry to join in the fun.' Rosalie rolled her eyes. 'He can be a bit of an old stick in the mud.'

They danced away. Evie bit her lip.

'What are you doing?' Uncle Sal asked Frances as he and Aunt Mildred returned to the bar.

'Waiting for your order,' Frances said. 'I wasn't sure if you'd like cocktails or champagne.'

She'd decided to stick to soda water. Let others consider her a wet blanket, she'd rather not make boozing a habit. A Mimosa or a glass of wine every day could easily become a bottle or two if one didn't watch it.

The bartender reached for his cocktail shaker. 'Your usual, Mrs Clifton?' he asked.

'Something more refreshing tonight, I think. Surprise me.'

Aunt Mildred dabbed her brow with a handkerchief. Tommy came rushing, handing her the fan. 'That's better, thank you,' she said. 'This costume is delightful but remind me to pick something cooler for the next ball.'

The bartender filled a cocktail glass with a pink concoction and added a cocktail cherry to it.

Evie signalled them they'd leave the table. Jack picked up a tray with champagne, soda water and glasses and sat down. Frances and the others followed him.

'Do you mind?' Jack asked as he reached for his holster.

'Hold it, cowboy,' a man behind him drawled. Frances recognized Mr Callaghan, an unlikely Tarzan in a knee-length brown dress, leaving one shoulder free. He brandished a rubber spear.

Jack produced his precious camera.

Mr Callaghan dropped his histrionic posture. 'I say, that's neat. I assume you're planning on taking our pictures?'

'Only if that's okay with you.'

'Anytime, old chap.' He smote Tommy on the back. 'I hardly recognised you without your glad rags. How about we all pose for our cowboy here?'

Jack snapped picture after picture, not just of his

company, but of the crowd as well. Rosalie and her fiancé, her mother as Isadora Duncan and one of the professional dancers as a pharaoh, Mr Forsythe watching from the sidelines, dressed as yet another pirate. He seemed a bit camera-shy, or maybe he thought Jack was taking liberties. As soon as he saw Jack's camera trained on himself, he disappeared in the crowd.

Most pictures though were of Frances. She'd overcome her original reluctance and posed happily in her costume.

'How are we getting hold of a photograph? Are you developing them yourself?' Mr Callaghan asked. Frances had wondered the same. Mum would be over the moon if she could send her a picture or two as an early Christmas present.

'I'll take the rolls to a studio in Bombay, run by an old mate,' Jack said. 'We're going to stop there for long enough to get the job done.'

He slipped the camera into his holster and said to Frances, 'I'll just put it away in my cabin and then we'll dance.'

Mr Callaghan and Tommy made their move simultaneously, asking Frances for a hop. Tommy instantly demurred, but to Frances surprise, Mr Callaghan did so as well and asked Tommy's aunt instead.

'He's much nicer tonight than I thought he'd be,' Frances said to her dance partner.

'Who, Callaghan? I wouldn't put too much store in his changed attitude. He probably had it brought home to him that making a blister of oneself in front of a few hundred people is a bad idea.'

Tommy swirled her around and right in the way of Evie and Lawrence Vaughan who exchanged a few quiet words.

Frances wondered if her friend was unwell. She seemed shaky, and her face changed colour. Lawrence Vaughan's face had a peculiar expression. Could it be pity for the girl whose feelings were so obvious?

His future mother-in-law slightly shook her head at him as she swished past. In return, he gave her a tiny shrug.

Tommy frowned. 'Bad show, that. Sorry, I shouldn't have said that.'

Frances simply smiled, unsure if an answer was required. She sighed with relief as Uncle Sal took over from Tommy. Here at least were no complicated society rules she might break out of ignorance.

'They're playing our song.' It was hard to make out Uncle Sal's expression under his thick face-paint, but his eyes sparkled. "How Come You Do Me Like You Do" had been the last vaudeville song he'd used in his stage act and the first one he and Frances had secretly rehearsed to when he came to live with her family.

Jack waved at her from the table before he led Aunt Mildred to the dance floor, past Ada and her not too ardent admirer. His infatuation, if it ever existed, had been short-lived, judging by the correct distance he kept between them during the dance.

Frances listened to the lyrics, tempted to sing along. The tune would have suited Evie's style, she thought, but the singer on stage with his velvety baritone was something else. He had the same star quality Uncle Sal had. It was more than only his voice, it felt as if every part of him lived the music. Uncle Sal held her closer, so their cheeks almost touched.

'How do you enjoy the travelling life?'

'I wish it would never end.' She sighed. 'This whole voyage is perfect.'

The song ended. 'I'd better return you to Jack,' Uncle Sal said. 'Nothing like young love to dance the night away.'

Old love too, Frances thought as Uncle Sal made a beeline for Aunt Mildred. Tonight, there seemed to be romance in the air.

'Where's the bastard? I'll wring his neck!' A beetle-red pirate jostled them out of the way. There were so many men wearing identical costumes that Frances had trouble telling them apart.

Mr Mackie, who'd just sat down at their table for the promised drink, rose from his seat and stopped the man. Face to face, they looked so alike in their costumes that Frances wondered if this too was part of the show. Applause from a couple of bystanders told her they agreed.

The angry pirate calmed down as Mr Mackie whispered a few words into his ear. He stomped off, to join Mr Fitch and Mr Brown. 'Total and utter rotter,' were the last things Frances heard before the music drowned out everything else.

∼

Frances still lay in bed, reliving every moment from last night, as the commotion broke out. A woman shrieked, followed by heavy footfall from the deck above hers, where the first-class suites were to be found.

She threw her shabby bathrobe over and tied it firmly around her waist before she peeked out of her cabin. A young steward hurried past; Sam, the young boy who looked after Uncle Sal and Jack.

'What's wrong?' she asked.

'I couldn't say, Miss.' He blinked like a startled horse. 'It's one of the passengers, that's all I know.'

Loud crying made Sam spin around. Evie sobbed in Nancy's arms. Frances rushed towards them, heedless of her own state of dishabille.

Nancy hugged Evie. 'He's dead,' she said to Frances, her voice reflecting more disbelief than anything else.

'Who is?' Suddenly, Frances became aware of her lack of proper clothing. 'Let's take Evie to my cabin. And, Sam, please bring us some brandy, and coffee.'

They both supported Evie who walked in a daze between them. As they were safely in Frances's cabin, she asked again. 'Who is dead?'

'It's Larry,' Evie said. She burst into fresh tears. 'But that's impossible. How could it be true?'

CHAPTER TWELVE

'It's true,' Jack said as Frances joined him and Uncle Sal for lunch. Evie had recovered from her shock after a large brandy and two aspirins, and she and Nancy had returned to work. Death or no death, dance lessons had to go on.

'When Lawrence Vaughan skipped morning tea, his fiancée sent Merry to rouse him. When there was no answer, he opened the cabin with his pass key and found Vaughan in his bed, dead.' Jack took a bite out of his sandwich. He'd seen enough on the battlefields to treat the passing of a man matter-of-factly.

Frances pushed her food away. 'How is that possible? He was a young man.'

'I assume the ship's doctor will examine him.' Jack put his hand on top of hers. 'It's sad, kiddo, but these things happen. Only because somebody is young and appears to be strong, he can still have a weak heart or another illness that no one suspected.'

'His poor fiancée. She must be distraught,' Frances said. 'And poor Evie.'

Jack and Uncle Sal exchanged an uncomfortable glance. 'It's a bad situation all around,' Uncle Sal said. 'If there's anything we can do for the girl, I'm in.'

By now the news must have spread all over the ship, because respectful silence fell as the Halsalls slowly made their way through the dining room. Both were dressed in black, although their fashionable silk frocks had not been made for mourning but for night-time revelries. Rosalie's skin was drained of any colour and her eyes were as red-rimmed as her mother's. The loss must have hit them both hard.

The captain made one of his rare appearances. He bent over the hand of the bereaved fiancée. 'My condolences,' he said. 'It's a tragedy for this to happen.'

'Thank you.' Rosalie's voice was a mere whisper. Her mother dabbed her eyes with a lace-edged handkerchief bearing her embroidered initials. 'It's been a terrible shock.'

'If there's anything at all we can do to help you through this ordeal, a word from you will do. My First Officer will see to it.' He gave a curt nod as Mr Whalan took over.

Mrs Halsall clasped Mr Whalan's hand. 'When will we be allowed to say our good-byes?'

'I'll ask the doctor. If you're sure you want to subject yourself to that ordeal?' The First Officer raised his brows in a manner that increased his resemblance to Gary Cooper. 'It might be distressful for you.'

'We need to say farewell to darling Larry,' Mrs Halsall said. 'It's having a few quiet moments with a loved one that gives you strength. I assure you that dear Rosalie and I are no strangers to loss, with my dear husband passing away much too soon.'

A small bark made several hands turn. Aunt Mildred had the grace to look abashed as she scooped up Tinkerbell and handed him to her nephew. Jack pulled out a chair for them.

She approached the Halsalls with outstretched hands. 'Doreen, dearest, and darling Rosalie. Such devastating news. If there's anything I can do?'

She kissed the air next to Doreen Halsall's cheeks in yet another of those society niceties that Frances had never encountered before.

'That's too kind of you, Mildred. Rosalie's simply heartbroken. I only hope that people will be kind when we arrive in London.' Her voice caught. 'I can't bear the idea that anybody could say a bad word about our wonderful Lawrence.'

'They won't,' Aunt Mildred said with an air of faint bewilderment. 'He'll be remembered as he was, a gentleman gone too soon. I assume you've sent a telegram to the family?'

'Not yet.' Rosalie's skin went even paler. 'I don't know what to write.'

'Or where they are, in town or at their country estate, while the hunting season is still on.'

Frances thought she'd heard a note of satisfaction in Doreen Halsall's voice, as if the social status of her daughter's dead fiancé reflected on them.

'Send it to both addresses,' Aunt Mildred said. She air-kissed the other woman again. 'And please, don't hesitate to call on me. The steward knows which cabin I'm in.'

She gave Rosalie's shoulder a gentle squeeze. 'Courage, my dear child.'

Tink wagged his tail stub as she sat down. He'd decided to climb onto Jack's lap while he waited for his food.

'What a terrible thing to happen.' Aunt Mildred rubbed her forehead. 'The girl seems to take it very hard, which only goes to show that these modern young things are not nearly as callous as they make out. And I don't remember Doreen being that cut up when her husband passed away. But then he'd been ailing for a while.'

She glanced at Rosalie who stirred a spoonful of a white powder from a small box into a glass of water. 'Bicarbonate of soda? The gal might have inherited her father's delicate stomach.'

Frances said, 'It must be awful to have to break the news.' She shivered. What if one of them had an accident? It would break her mother's heart if she couldn't be by their side in times of need. Suddenly, being in the middle of the ocean ceased being fun. Instead, it scared her.

Aunt Mildred reached for her pince-nez. 'Rosalie won't have any trouble finding a new match,' she declared after watching the colour and animation returning to Rosalie's face. 'She isn't well-connected enough to attract an American millionaire, because they all want a title in return for their cash, but she'll do nicely if she's willing to settle for a little less money and status than Lawrence Vaughan had to offer. Black suits her, too.'

Frances thought of Evie, who'd sobbed her heart out over the same man. 'He didn't look that important.' She cringed. 'I mean, he seemed nice enough, only not that different from the other first-class passengers.'

'Fourth in line to a baronetcy, and a family in private banking,' Tommy said. 'Nice chap, too. Not too much brains, as you might have noticed at the craps table, but I've never heard anything bad about him. Damn shame.'

'Had they been engaged long?' Frances said a silent thank you to Mr Wodehouse again. Without his preparation, she'd have wondered how everybody seemed to know each other in a metropolis like London. Instead, she accepted the fact that all the rich and noble folks were like a club, where everybody moved in the same circles. No wonder Evie couldn't compete.

'I think the notice was in the papers around Easter,' Aunt Mildred said.

They'd just finished their lunch when Nancy stumbled into the room. She ignored consternated frowns as she bumped into a couple on their way out.

'Frances?' Nancy's head swivelled as she tried to find her. Her mascara had smudged.

'Take her to the piano bar,' Jack said. 'The girl looks like she could do with a spot of privacy.'

Uncle Sal nudged her. 'We'll be on the observation deck, if you need us.'

In the passage, Frances and Nancy brushed past Mr Whalan who stood with his feet planted wide and an unyielding face. Nancy shot him a pleading look that puzzled Frances, unless Evie had betrayed her feelings for the late Lawrence Vaughan, and Nancy hoped that the First Officer could somehow stop rumours from spreading.

The piano bar was too full for her liking, with Mr Callaghan and Mr Fitch both glaring a hole in Mr Forsythe's broad back.

Nancy shrank back as she saw them. Frances took her to the library instead, which at this hour was empty apart from two elderly ladies who were deaf to the world as they devoured scandalous novels.

'Sit down and take a deep breath.'

Nancy obeyed as she slumped in the chair. 'I'm sorry I dragged you away from your friends,' she said. 'Only, I didn't know what else to do.'

'That's fine. Just tell me what's wrong.'

Nancy's lips trembled. 'They've taken Evie away.'

'What?' An icy chill crept over Frances's skin.

'Mr Mackie and the purser came as we were waiting for our dance students and asked her to come with them. It had something to do with Larry Vaughan.' Nancy bit her knuckles. 'I think she's in a lot of trouble.'

'Surely she hasn't done anything wrong?'

'Of course, she hasn't. But who'd believe that from a girl who's flinging her legs around on a stage for money?'

'We'll need to see Jack,' Frances said. 'He's friends with one of the stewards, and Mr Mackie owes him a favour too. If anyone can find out what's going on, it's him.'

'Do you really think so?' Nancy lowered her head. 'I have to go back to work. Ada will already be wondering what happened to me, on top of everything else.'

'Can you come to my cabin as soon as you're free?'

'That's when everyone's at afternoon tea.' She blew her nose and opened her compact to glance into the mirror. A shriek escaped her. 'Good heavens, I look like a scarecrow.'

Nancy dashed off, leaving a pensive Frances behind. What on earth could the First Officer suspect Evie of that they'd take her away?

Jack had the answer, when she found him watching the cricket.

'Your friend's in big trouble,' he said before she could speak a single word. 'It's about as bad as can be.'

'What kind of trouble?' She remembered Evie's expensive cigarette case, and other valuable items. They'd been presents, though. Did they think she'd stolen something from Larry Vaughan?

Jack lowered his voice so only she could hear him. 'The doctor didn't like what he saw. He believes our man was poisoned and that Evie Miles had something to do with it.'

'Murder?' Frances whispered. 'That's ridiculous. How could Evie kill him, and why?' White spots danced before her eyes.

CHAPTER THIRTEEN

'I've got you.' Jack steadied Frances as her vision normalised. 'You're white as a ghost. I shouldn't have sprung this on you.' He took her up to the open deck. All around them, there was nothing but rolling waves, and a pod of dolphins frolicking in the dazzling blue water. The sun flecked it golden. It should have been the most serene setting. Instead, Frances felt sick with nerves.

'I don't believe it,' she said.

Jack held her in his arms. Her heartbeat calmed down. Everything would be fine, as long as he was by her side.

'Which part? The murder or Evie's involvement?' His tone was neutral. This wasn't their first brush with crime, but usually they both agreed straight away when it came to the suspect.

'Evie,' she said. 'She's as nice as can be, and she really cared for him.'

'Maybe that's the problem. A poor girl from the lower classes who sets her sight on a man way above her station, who happens to also be engaged to be married.'

She stomped her feet. 'You make her sound cheap when you of all people should understand her. When it came to Merriweather, you never for one single moment believed he could have done something wrong.' Her voice wobbled. This was as close to having a fight as they'd ever come.

'I'm not judging her, kiddo,' he said as he cupped her chin. 'It's what everyone else will be saying, including the captain.'

'Then it's up to us to prove them wrong.'

'Once again.' Fine lines showed up in his face. It wasn't fair, she thought. For once, he was free of shouldering the responsibility for more than a dozen people, and here they were, forced by circumstances to go sleuthing once more.

'I'll try to get hold of Merry again,' he said. 'For now, though, it's best to mingle and keep our ears open.'

Uncle Sal reclined in a deck chair, with a tea tray next to him on a table. He swung his legs around to sit upright and patted the armrest for Frances to perch upon. Being close to him instantly cheered Frances up. Uncle Sal and Jack weren't only the nicest men she knew, they were also the smartest.

The cricket players stood huddled together, with Tommy in their midst. He shuffled his feet as he leant on his cricket bat.

'Your nephew seems uncomfortable,' Jack said to Aunt Mildred who occupied the deck chair next to Uncle Sal. Large sunshades covered her eyes, and an open magazine lay on her lap. Tink pressed his head into her side as he snored.

'Poor Tommy hates controversy,' she said.

Jack grinned. 'Not ideal if he's destined for the Foreign Office.'

She pushed the glasses down the bridge of her nose to peer at him. 'Diplomats don't have controversies, only differences of opinions, as you're perfectly well aware of.'

'Why aren't they playing?' Frances asked.

'Because it makes you appear a bit of a cad when you've tragically lost one of your own.'

'Yet they're dressed for cricket,' Frances said.

'It also takes a bit of courage to openly call off your afternoon sport, and I assume nobody wants to be the first.' She took one of the teacups. 'Would you be a dear and pour?'

As Frances handed her the filled cup, Aunt Mildred said, 'I think Tommy has suffered enough. Could you please summon him?'

Frances wanted to protest. After all, Aunt Mildred could easily call him herself, when she saw the brief wink aimed at her before the sunshades were pushed back in place.

She ambled over to the cricket area. Curious glances followed her. Either these people recognised her from their show, or from Nancy's upset appearance at lunch. She slowed down, careful to make it obvious she had no care in the world.

'Hello, Tommy?' She beamed at the cricket players.

He took a step back and trod onto Mr Fitch's toes. 'Awfully sorry, old chap,' he said to him. 'Hullo, Frances. I say, you're a sight for sore eyes.'

Another of the players ogled her so openly, her skin crawled. 'Why don't you introduce us to your lady friend?' the man asked.

Tommy's bow furrowed. 'Listen, chum –'

'Your aunt asked me to fetch you,' Frances said. 'Oh, and there's my fiancé.' She made a great show of waving to Jack.

'I'll be there in a tick,' Tommy promised.

The other man snickered. 'I'd rather chase a skirt than hide behind one.'

'You're an idiot,' Mr Fitch said, before Tommy could reply. 'If you can't hold your drink, you can at least shut up and stop embarrassing yourself. I'm sorry, Miss Palmer.'

'It's not your fault,' Francs said, mildly flattered that he knew her name.

Tommy set the unused cricket bat aside and hurried to leave the enclosure.

'I do apologise,' he said to Frances. 'Some of the boys have been drowning their sorrow over Larry a bit too early.'

'You haven't,' she said.

'Gosh, no. Doesn't help anyone, does it?' His cheeks reddened. 'I hope you don't think any worse of me.'

'She won't,' Aunt Mildred said. Tink opened one eye and yawned. 'Does my darling need a proper nap?' She kissed the silky head. 'I'd suggest we retire to my suite, so Tommy and I can change. I've ordered a few refreshments.'

Frances marvelled at the ease with which Aunt Mildred sailed through the crowd. Instead of trying to make herself small or constantly saying "Excuse me", like Frances would, people made way for her and her followers. It must be her imperious posture or her utter disregard for any obstacle.

Tommy too commandeered a new respect. She'd seen him blush and bumble, but he held himself with the same ease born of long practice. Like he simply had never considered anyone blocking his way.

Both he and Aunt Mildred disappeared into their separate dressing rooms, a luxury Frances had seen described in the brochure she intended to keep as a souvenir.

'Make yourself comfortable,' Aunt Mildred called out.

A tray with finger sandwiches and fancy little cakes stood ready on the sofa table, together with plates and coffee for five.

Aunt Mildred returned, massaging rose-scented cream into her hands. She'd changed her dress for a loose kaftan.

She knocked on Tommy's door. He opened, his white cricket pants changed for cream-coloured flannels.

'Finally,' she said. 'Now, tell me everything. What in earth is going on with Larry Vaughan?'

'He's still dead,' Tommy said.

She rolled her eyes. 'And there are all kinds of funny things going on, I've been told.'

'The boys say there was foul play,' Tommy said. 'Isn't that why you insisted on me playing cricket instead of shuffleboard?'

Aunt Mildred didn't bat an eyelid.

'Who told them?' Frances asked.

'It's true, then?' Tommy reached for the coffee, only to yelp. 'That's hot.'

Aunt Mildred shook his head at him as she gripped the pot by its handle. 'You're not supposed to touch the pot itself. Now, talk.'

'One of the boys saw the doctor coming out of Tommy's cabin. He said he looked waxen as hell.' Tommy winced.

'Pardon my language. Anyway, next thing the First Officer came running, which kind of set the cat among the pigeons. I mean, they'd already established Larry was a goner, right?'

'I wondered why he didn't call for help. Is there any way to alarm the steward during the night?' Jack asked.

Aunt Mildred harrumphed. 'You would have thought so. No, if there's anything you need, you have to take care of things before you retire or wait until the morning.'

'These chaps are run off their feet already,' Tommy said. 'The last thing they need is to be summoned at all hours because one of the old birds has used up his last match and wants another cigarette before going to sleep.'

'But there must be some emergency system for the first-class passengers,' Frances said, strangely disappointed to find a flaw in the system.

'They obviously expect you to be able to make it to the door and call out, or otherwise travel with your own nurse' Aunt Mildred said.

'Only Larry Vaughan didn't come out.' Uncle Sal bit into a salmon and cucumber sandwich.

'Which is why the boys decided there is something deuced fishy about the whole affair,' Tommy said.

'And what do they believe happened?' Jack asked.

'They're not sure, but it seems there as a bit of a dust-up over that pretty red-head.' Tommy winced again. 'Miss Miles, I mean.'

'With whom? Callaghan?'

'He, and the older bloke, Forsythe. But for my money, it had to do with the gambling.'

'Why? Did Larry owe money?' Jack and Uncle Sal spoke in unison.

'He used to be pretty lucky until lately, when he was distracted the whole time. The boys think he was blackmailed over something, maybe the girl, and that he threatened to pipe up. Fitch and Sanders swear there was something rotten at the gambling tables too. That's why Sanders made such a stink last night.'

Frances, Jack and Uncle Sal exchanged a puzzled glance.

'The pirate?' Tommy asked. 'The one out for blood? That was Sanders. Callaghan thinks so too. He and Forsythe used to be chummy, but two nights ago, that changed.'

'What happened two nights ago?'

'I wish I knew,' Tommy said. 'But it seems pretty clear to me that there was an awful lot of weird stuff going on that Larry got caught up in. And then he died.'

CHAPTER FOURTEEN

Jack adjusted his collar as Merry arrived. 'Sorry to drag you away from your duties,' he said. 'What do you know about the Vaughan case?'

Merry pursed his lips as if to whistle. 'You're interested?'

'That depends on what's going on. There's talk of foul play.'

'The doctor has been asking questions about rat poison, so something is up.'

'What's that got to do with Evie Miles?'

Merry's mouth opened in surprise. 'The entertainer?'

'Mr Whalan and the purser seem to hold something against her.'

'I haven't heard anything yet but leave it to me. She's a nice kid.'

'I appreciate it. When do you come off duty?'

'I usually have a last cigarette outside at midnight. There's a sheltered corner next to the lifeboats.'

Rosalie and her mother were missing from the dining room. Their table stayed empty, and people gave it a wide miss as if tragedy was contagious.

Only Mr Callaghan and his friends moved directly past it. Mr Sanders touched Larry Vaughan's deserted chair and scowled at Mr Forsythe as he marched towards their table.

'That's pretty damning behaviour from a swell cove,' Uncle Sal said. 'I wonder what's causing all that bad blood.'

'It's not the done thing.' Tommy agreed. 'Either Sanders has something to say about Forsythe, and then he should either take it up with him or the captain, or he should act civil. You must get a bad impression of us Englishmen, Frances.'

'Not at all,' Frances said. 'Nobody else seemed to mind anyway.'

'Too busy with their dinner,' Jack said. 'I'm sure Sanders would be only too happy to share his burden with a sympathetic listener.'

'Gossip makes the world go around.' Aunt Mildred signalled for a glass of wine. 'I have complete faith in your sense of diplomacy, Tommy dearest.'

Nancy and Ada only showed themselves after dinner. Their faces wore more paint than usual, and their smiles stretched their lips too thin, without reaching their eyes. Still, to a casual observer they would seem fine as they laughed at their dance partners observations.

'Where's the other one?' One of the older men asked a steward.

'I couldn't say, sir.' Did the man stiffen a little? Frances earwigged shamelessly, to hear Nancy say, 'Miss Miles is inconvenienced tonight.' The dancer grimaced and rubbed her tummy, indicating indigestion. The steward lowered his head the fraction of an inch, as if to confirm Nancy said the right thing.

Frances's stretched nerves relaxed a little. Whatever was happening, at least things were hushed up for now.

The orchestra played a foxtrot. Never in a million years had Frances imagined that dancing with Jack could be anything but heaven, but she had to concentrate on the steps.

'Cheer up,' he murmured. 'We'll have more information before the night is out.'

Despite his words Jack too seemed distracted. When Mr Callaghan and Mr Fitch excused themselves, he handed Frances over to Aunt Mildred and asked Uncle Sal to go for a liquid refreshment with him.

A look at his face told Frances that Jack had a plan, and that she should stay where she was.

Tommy had taken his instructions seriously and plied Mr Sanders with a cocktail at the bar.

Aunt Mildred pressed her fingertips against her temples. 'Shall we leave? It's such a bore to wait for someone and the music is hurting my head.'

'Shall we leave a message?'

'My nephew can be relied upon, and your men will be aware where to search for you.'

Frances agreed. She longed for a cooling breeze after the close air inside. 'A stroll on deck might ease your headache.'

Aunt Mildred laughed. 'It might, although you probably deserve better company than an old woman like me under a starlit sky.'

'Nonsense,' Frances said, although secretly she agreed with the observation. 'Shall we collect Tinkerbell?'

~

Five men led by Mr Sanders held a heated meeting close to the staircase as Frances and Aunt Mildred passed through the door. The women ignored them. They were too busy fussing over their hair in the wind in Aunt Mildred's case, and holding Tink on his leash in Frances's case. At least she hoped that's what it appeared like. Her only regret was that she had no excuse to take a geek and see if she recognised the other men.

Aunt Mildred sank onto a deck chair in the shadow. Frances followed her example. Arranging her chair allowed her to see the men close enough to identify Mr Fitch and Mr Brown. Tink snuggled up to her. She shushed him, intent on hearing whatever went on among the men.

It was depressingly little. Mr Sanders tried to convince the other four to march to the captain's cabin and demand information and the locking up of all the suspects.

Mr Fitch, the least sozzled of them, argued that they should wait until the morning. 'The captain will be giving us the bum's rush if we break into his bedroom, smelling like a boozer. And lock up who?'

'That stinker, Forsythe. For one. He's been giving old Larry the evil eye more than enough.' Mr Sanders burst into hiccups.

'What about the doll?' The man who'd ogled Frances earlier piped up.

'Are you crazy, Stinker?' Mr Brown slapped Mr Sanders

on the back. 'Miss Halsall is a lady.'

'Not her. The one with the legs up to her chin.' Stinker made a lewd gesture.

'Don't be stupid. Why would she do away with Larry?' Mr Sanders sounded almost sober now, after the hiccups. 'Girls like that are used to being a bit of fun on the side. If Larry would have gone that far, which I doubt, with his fiancée and her mama around.'

Frances bristled at his word choice.

Aunt Mildred looked as if she agreed with Mr Sanders. Her dog did not, because he woofed.

'Let's have another snifter before the bar closes,' one of the men said. They staggered inside.

'Sleep is a good idea,' Aunt Mildred said and reached for Tink.

~

A glowing point and the smell of burning tobacco led Jack to Merry's hideout. The steward lounged on a chair next to the lifeboats. His eyes had lost their twinkle, but that could be due to the fatigue which was obvious to Jack. Being on your feet all day and having to appear unwaveringly cheerful took its toll. It could be hard enough on his staff at the Top Note, and they took shifts on busy nights.

Merry offered Jack his case with Turkish cigarettes and lit one for him. 'Makes you go all cold inside, seeing a stiff in peace-times,' he said.

'Where is the body? Still in the surgery?'

'Doc's finished a while ago. You haven't met him yet, have you? Nice bloke, and good at his job too.'

'I don't think I've had the pleasure.'

Merry chuckled. 'The poor man's been hiding. One of the first-class passengers has become a bit keen. First, she discovered a new ache or symptom every day since Bombay, until Doc Gifford mentioned he'd like to send her to the hospital in Sydney for further testing. He hasn't shown his face in the dining room ever since.' He took a deep drag. 'Anyway, the body is now in the cooling storage, in a coffin. We're not advertising that fact. It might make people squeamish when it comes to their dinner.'

'Fair enough,' Jack said. 'What did he say?'

Merry stubbed out the cigarette in a metal ashtray. 'He's sure it was poison. Probably arsenic, from the rat poison we have in our pantry.'

Jack flinched, although he'd expected this answer. 'Who has access to the pantry?'

'Everyone on our staff. You don't need to work in the kitchen to pop in for a snack or a chat. And it gets worse for the kid.' Merry grimaced. 'Mr Whalan took her into custody because they found a few things belonging to the girl in Mr Vaughan's cabin. A feather from her dress and under a chair, her cigarette case. He must have kicked it there when he was thrashing out, poor bastard.'

'I see.'

'There was a piece of fabric too, with sequins, that must have been snatched in a drawer. The cabin boy swears it wasn't there in the morning but even if that happened during an earlier visit, the feather could only have come off the dress that night. It had never been worn before.'

'They could be the fiancée's. Has that been checked?'

'I'll ask Mr Whalan.'

CHAPTER FIFTEEN

'Are you sure the cigarette case belonged to Evie?' Frances's stomach twisted itself into a knot.

'That's at least what the captain thinks.'

'But they're sold here on the ship.'

'Which means we need to discover if anyone else bought an identical one, and if Evie can lay hand on hers.' Jack finished his last forkful of kedgeree. Frances had stuck with porridge. It had a comforting effect on her because it reminded her of her childhood, when a bowl of porridge would start a day when nothing bad could happen.

'Mildred and I'll tackle the shops,' Uncle Sal said. 'She's itching to do something, and upper-crust enough that nobody will think twice about not falling over themselves to answer any question coming from her.'

He tapped his fingers on the table to a melody in his head only he could hear. Some of Frances's worries melted away. As long as they had a plan and ideas, nothing could go wrong. Unless – she hushed her voice. 'Where are they holding her?'

She'd visited Adelaide prison once, and that had been bad enough although the wardens were friendly. Being imprisoned on a ship sounded much worse. It conjured up images of manacles, windowless cells and rats scurrying across filthy floors, despite the lack of any evidence she had that the *Empress of the Sea* housed any vermin or lacked cleanliness.

Her mouth went dry. She gulped down her tea.

'She's in an empty cabin,' Jack said.

'Can I visit her?'

'I'll ask Merry if it's possible to arrange a chat with Captain Grey.' Jack stroked her arm. 'In the meantime, try to talk to the other dancers, or mingle to hear the gossip.'

~

Frances and Uncle Sal went through their rehearsal as quickly as they could. Skipping it was out of the question because it formed an unwritten part of their contract. After dropping the juggling balls twice, Frances managed to shut out every other thought. Uncle Sal had mastered that trick in his youth, but then he'd never been found without total concentration and a blinding smile no matter how tough the circumstances.

Ada and Nancy had not quite reached that stage. Although their eyes were dry as they tapped on their high heels into the ball room, their heavy use of powder and rouge only partly covered their paleness.

Frances gave Uncle Sal a brief nod. 'Have fun with Aunt Mildred.' He bowed in perfect stage manner and took himself off with a wave to the dancers.

'How are you?' Frances asked.

Ada's tap shoes clacked as she did a series of complicated steps that somehow looked effortless.

Nancy copied the moves, loud enough to give them cover. 'I can't believe it,' she said. 'I tried to tell Mr Mackie that Evie would never do anything wrong, and he just shrugged. I mean, he didn't even try to pretend he believed me.'

'And we're under strict orders to come up with a new dance number to entertain the crowd. The show must go on.' Ada imitated Mr Mackie in a less than flattering manner. 'As if the passengers would write letters to the company if they get stiffed out of Evie's routine.'

'They wouldn't let me go to her.' Nancy's lip wobbled as she tapped away. 'I only wanted to bring her a change of clothes and her hairbrush. Heaven knows where they've put her.'

'It's crazy.' Ada paused and gave Nancy a critical glance. 'You've got the wrong step, honey. It's a pick-up, not a shuffle.'

'She's in a cabin of her own.' Frances rubbed the bridge of her nose. 'What's the harm with you bringing Evie a few things?'

'Like I said, crazy. It's not like we could break her out, not thousands of miles from shore.'

'What do you think happened to Larry Vaughan?' Frances asked.

'Heart attack,' Ada said with an air of finality. 'It hits young men too. My second cousin was out delivering coal in London one morning, and just like that, he dropped dead.' She snapped her fingers for illustration. 'Thirty-four and strong like an ox, his mum said.'

'The doctor would have said if it was a faulty ticker.' Nancy shook her gleaming curls. 'I bet it would all have been hushed up if not for Mrs Halsall. If Doc Gifford is sure of foul play, then I believe him. Only they got the wrong suspect.'

'Who would want to kill Larry Vaughan?' Frances frowned.

'And why?' Ada clapped her hands. 'I've got it. What if somebody stole into his cabin during the night and disturbed Larry? The murderer had to silence him.'

'Was there anything worth stealing?'

'Cash and his jewellery. He had real diamonds in his cufflinks and a signet ring handed down over generations,' Evie said. And if he won a bundle at cards or at the crap table, it'd be in his cabin.'

'True, but how would anyone else get inside?' Nancy sighed.

'Locks aren't that hard to pick.' The words flew out of Frances's mouth before she could stop herself.

Nancy's mouth firmed an astonished o. 'Do you do those tricks where someone is chained up and has to escape?'

Frances thought as fast as she could. What if the dancers spread the news that Salvatore the Magnificent and his assistant could pick locks? They had one act where they used handcuffs, but maybe they should shelve it.

'No,' she said. 'Uncle Sal used to work with people who did those kinds of performances, and he met Harry

Houdini a few times.' Enough truth to keep Nancy and Ada satisfied and not enough to start rumours.

'The person could have hidden in the closet and waited until Larry went to sleep,' Ada suggested.

'Wait.' Nancy stopped her tap routine for a beat until Ada nudged her. 'Didn't somebody say he was poisoned? Maybe the killer spiked his drink and hid in the cabin until Larry was dead before he made off with the valuables.' She gulped. 'That's horrible, waiting for a man to die.'

Frances hadn't considered that possibility. 'Why would the captain think Evie had something to do with his death?' It would be interesting if word about the evidence tying their friends to the scene of the crime had reached the girls.

Ada and Nancy exchanged a meaningful look.

'You're not going to tell anyone? Apart from your menfolk?' Ada crossed her arms over her chest.

'Of course not. But we can only help if we have the information we need.'

'Evie and Larry used to be – friendly. If you understand.'

'And his fiancée?' Even in her own ears, the words came out prissy.

Ada rolled her eyes. 'He embarked alone in Colombo and took a few dance lessons on the way. Talk about love at first sight. He conveniently forgot to mention he was getting shackled until they joined him in Australia, where they'd visited family. When Evie found out, the cat was properly among the pigeons and she gave him the heave-ho before you could say, scram.'

'Not that there had been much going on,' Nancy said. 'A

few moonlight strolls and a kiss or two, that's all. Let people say what they want, Evie is a decent girl.'

'It must have been terrible for her.' How would Frances have felt if Jack's former love turned up out of the blue? And Rosalie was the fiancée which made it twice as hurtful for both of them. 'How could he do that?'

'I can't blame him if he forgot all about that toffee-nosed lady and her stuck-up mother. Not much love lost between them, I thought.' Ada snorted.

'It would have been fine if he'd stopped hanging out around us,' Nancy said. 'But no, he'd ask Evie to dance or watch her, making sheep's eyes when she did any of her routines. Only a blind woman would not have noticed anything.'

'It's not as if Evie told him to get lost.' Ada rubbed her calf. 'Too nice by half and the poor kid was still sweet on him.' She stopped and stared at Frances. 'Which I've never said if anybody asks me.'

'I understand.'

'Good. Blimey, what an awful mess this is.'

CHAPTER SIXTEEN

Uncle Sal listened to Mildred's portable gramophone while she changed into a sleuthing outfit, as she called it. Tommy was already on the job, keeping an eye on Mr Sanders and his friends.

He hummed along to Josephine Baker's "J'ai Deux Amours". Imported records cost a fortune in Australia. Maybe he should splurge when they arrived in London and buy a gramophone and some music as a Christmas present for the family. Although, when Frances and Jack married, he doubted that her mother would stay in Adelaide. With her son and two grandchildren up in Queensland, nobody could blame her if she wanted to be close to them.

He wouldn't mention that thought to Frances. She'd only fret about him needlessly. He could take care of himself. He always had, before he moved in with the Palmers.

Mildred flounced into the room as the music ended. 'What do you say?' She slung a mink stole around her shoulders and lifted her chin.

He grinned. 'You look like a duchess ready to crush commoners under your heel.' With the return of her haughtiest stare and an abundance of purple silk and pearls, she'd converted back to the slightly frightening woman he'd taken her for at their first meeting.

She snatched her gloves. 'Good. Let's go before I melt in this fur.'

'You could take it off.'

'Ha. Nothing says rich like fur when there is absolutely no need for it.'

Uncle Sal agreed with that sentiment when he saw the shop assistant's instant awe. The girl curtsied before the door had closed behind them.

Mildred took out her pince-nez and scanned the silver flasks, vanity cases, powder puffs, barrettes and cigarette cases inside the glass cabin. 'Is that all you have to offer?' she asked in a tired tone.

'Indeed not, madam. We keep our more valuable merchandise locked away. Is there anything in particular I could show you?'

Mildred scrutinised the items again. 'I do wonder if I should wait until Bombay. They do have charming little trinkets there. Or there's always Bond Street in London.'

Uncle Sal stepped up to her. 'That is a nice vanity case, with the mother-of-pearl inlay,' he said.

'I assume it's not too bad.' She took a loser look before she honoured the shop assistant with her attention. 'What else do you have for me?'

The young woman unhooked a keyring from her belt and unlocked a drawer.

'These are straight from Paris,' she said as she put a cloth-covered tray on the counter.

Mildred leant over it and picked up a golden vanity case with jet stripes forming an asymmetric design. She snapped it open. Inside were five compartments. 'That is quite nice,' she said as she weighed it in her hand. '24 carat plating?'

The shop assistant paused for an awkward moment.

'Never mind, dear.' Mildred gave her a flicker of a smile. The young woman breathed easier. 'I assume you have more copies of this model?'

'Oh, no, madam. It's much too expensive to stock many. Maybe you're looking for something a little less exclusive?'

'You mean cheap?' Mildred arched her eyebrows. She radiated frostiness.

The shop assistant gulped until Mildred's face softened. 'I understand your concern and applaud you. What about those cigarette cases?' She addressed Uncle Sal. 'I'd like your opinion, as a man. What would my nephew like? I want it to be a surprise.'

Uncle Sal made a show of studying the various items, with their leather, gold or silver casing. Some were plain and mass-produced. Those he discarded straight away. After a little deliberation, he set two aside. One was silver, with engraved swirls, identical to Evie's case, apart from the gemstone in the clasp. This one had a topaz. The second case was made of gold embossed in a diamond pattern.

He held them both up to the light. 'These ones,' he said. 'They're distinctive but not flashy.'

'Excellent choice.' The shop assistant showed him her

dimples in what must be her normal sales pitch. 'The craftsmanship really shows in the details.'

'But how would one tell them apart? I assume you sell lots of them, and the young men all mingle at the bars and the gaming tables,' Mildred said.

'We never have more than a dozen copies of anything we sell,' the shop assistant said.

'That's still a lot.' Mildred tapped a finger to her lips. 'You can do monogramming, I presume?'

'We certainly can. Most people ask for a monogram when they purchase them as a gift.'

Mildred picked up the silver case. 'Does it ever happen that people ask for the same initials?'

The shop assistant giggled. 'Not since the last trip, it hasn't. And then they both selected the same gemstone in the clasp too.'

'How very unfortunate. How many of each model do you stock?'

'Only three.'

'So, you've got topaz left and what else?'

'One emerald and one sapphire.'

'No ruby?' Uncle Sal asked. 'They're supposed to be lucky.'

The shop assistant lifted her shoulders in regret. 'The last one sold three days ago.'

'Do you remember who purchased it?' Mildred asked. 'If it's a lady, there's hardly a chance Tommy would have an opportunity to muddle the cases up. But it if it was a gentleman ...' She sighed, overcome by the difficulty.

'I can't say, madam. I'm sorry. It was during my lunch break –'

'Which is at what time?'

'Two o'clock, madam. We keep the sales receipts in our ledger, and that's how I know it was sold.'

Mildred ran her finger over the expensive vanity case. 'If you'd be a dear and ask your colleague if she remembers? And please set the vanity case and those two cigarette cases aside for me. I'll come back when I've made up my mind.'

'Nice piece of work,' Uncle Sal said as soon as they were outside.

She flung off her mink stole and thrust it into his hand. 'And not a moment too soon. They do use the heating generously on this ship.' True enough, the other shoppers wore short sleeves and skimpy skirts or lightweight pants.

Mildred slipped her arm through his. 'Now we've earned our lunch.'

Tommy and Tinkerbell were already in the dining room. He jumped up to pull out a chair for his aunt. A wide grin split his face almost in two.

'Thank you, darling.' His aunt patted his hand. 'Shall we wait for the rest?'

Frances hurried along. 'Where's Jack?'

'Not here yet. We can wait with our order.'

'That won't be necessary.' Jack turned up behind her and touched her shoulder.

They took their after-lunch coffee in a secluded corner in the piano bar. The music tinkled softly, quiet enough for them to talk, loud enough to mask their voices from others.

'Captain Grey has agreed to a visit with your friend. One of his men will stay with you,' Jack said.

Frances opened her mouth to protest and then thought

better of it. It might help Evie's cause to show she had nothing to hide. 'Bonzer. I'll ask her if she has any idea who might have hated Larry, and if she can put hands on her cigarette case.'

'That's the spirit,' Aunt Mildred said. 'We know there are two other cases with a ruby set into the clasp, and that the last one was purchased recently. With any luck, the shop assistant can find out the name of the buyer.'

'What about the green feather and the fabric?' Frances asked. 'We need to discover if they could have come from another frock.'

'Not Rosalie's,' Aunt Mildred said. 'That girl sticks to black, white, gold and silver.'

'It might have been a new addition to her wardrobe,' Frances said. 'There were a few ladies changing their minds forever over the masquerade.'

Uncle Sal chortled. 'Shall I accompany Milady to the dressmakers?'

'Is nobody going to ask me anything?' Tommy almost sounded annoyed.

'Of course, dear. Do tell,' his aunt said.

'I can tell you that Larry Vaughan intended to raise an almighty stink together with his chum Sanders, because he said he saw the so-called major cheat at craps.' That got everyone's attention, to Tommy's gratitude.

'How could he tell?' Jack asked. He'd seen his share of fraud at the gambling tables, and a man like Forsythe could be counted upon to be slick.

'You've noticed how some men spit in their hands for luck or rattle the dice in their cupped hands, with their eyes shut?'

'Let me guess.' Uncle Sal slammed the table. 'He had his hands up high enough to let the dice slide into his sleeves. When he brought them down, out came a crooked set.' He paused. 'Would that work?'

'He had them in his handkerchief. Blew his nose and hey presto, a new pair of dice, one that netted him a nice big bundle.'

'That's a new trick to me,' Jack said. 'So, how did Larry Vaughan spot the switch?'

'Sheer dumb luck. One of the old dice had a tiny bit of black missing on the three eyes. He was just going to suggest getting a new set of dice from the steward when suddenly the flaw was gone after Forsythe handled the dice.'

'Why didn't Larry say anything straight away?' Frances drummed her fingertips on the table. She itched to talk to Evie, and yet she couldn't tear herself away.

'Because it's not the kind of thing that comes natural to a public-school man,' Tommy said. 'Only when Sanders thought it fishy as well, how much luck the major appeared to have when the stakes were raised, did he mention it in private.'

'Then Forsythe would have had no idea they were onto him.' Frances deflated. 'That means he had no motive.'

'Not so fast,' Jack said. 'Larry Vaughan struck me as a pleasant, well-bred young man, but not exactly the type who could hide their feelings. Con artists have a sixth sense for anything threatening their hide.'

'That's what Sanders said. And he made it clear at the costume ball that he thought Forsythe was up to no good.'

Aunt Mildred clapped her hands. 'Bravo, Tommy dear.

Now all you have to do is keep your ears open for any more gossip.'

He mock-saluted her. 'Yes, madam.'

'There's one more man you shouldn't overlook,' Uncle Sal said.

'There is?' Aunt Mildred asked.

'You're right.' Frances's pulse quickened. 'Callaghan also had a fall-out with Larry Vaughan, and with Forsythe, because they were all sweet in Evie. And he has a nasty temper. Otherwise he wouldn't have tried to pick a fight with Tommy.'

'He's a coward, too.' Jack flashed her a grin. 'His blood cooled off fast enough when he saw I meant business.'

'Poison is a coward's weapon.' Aunt Mildred waved Tommy closer. 'What are you waiting for, my dear?'

CHAPTER SEVENTEEN

The cabin that served as Evie's prison was a deck below Frances's quarters. The broad-shouldered sailor who had orders to stick to her throughout unlocked the door. 'Wait here, Miss,' he told her.

She could hear murmured instructions. The cabin was one of two at the end of a dingy corridor, behind a row of storage rooms. Frances wondered if this was the usual lock-up for sailors who did something wrong. It would make sense, because nobody would have a reason to be in this area except for a quick visit. On the far end of the long corridor were laundry and scullery. Both were the sole domain of lascars, Frances had been told.

The sailor beckoned Frances inside.

She had practised a bright smile that slipped as she saw Evie. The girl sat behind a table covered by a floor-length tablecloth. A water jug and a plate with half-eaten sandwiches assured Frances that her friend suffered no neglect, but her skin had lost its sheen and her eyes were sunk in their sockets. A folding screen hid what Frances assumed to be the sleeping part of the cabin, and a small bathroom.

'How are you?' she asked. 'Has the doctor been to see you?'

'I'm fine, Frances.' Evie wrung her hands in a nervous motion. 'It's only this whole situation that's driving me crazy.'

'We'll get you out of here,' Francs said. 'I promise.'

The sailor cleared his throat.

'Ignore him.' Frances leant over the table. 'You're innocent and we're going to prove it.'

'How? I don't understand what's going on.' Evie hung her head.

Frances hated to bring it up. 'There was your past relationship with Larry. I think that's the worst bit. And then there was some stuff of yours found in his cabin.'

'What are you talking about? I've been inside his cabin exactly once, before we reached Australia.' A faint pink tinged her throat. 'I stayed less than ten minutes, to help him decide on an outfit. I swear to God, Frances.'

'I believe you. And I believe that somebody planted evidence to make it appear like you murdered him.'

Evie choked. 'How did he die?'

'Poison. That's all the information we have so far.'

Tears sprang into Evie's eyes. 'How awful. Did he suffer much?'

Frances had no idea, but the whole affair was gruesome enough without setting off their imagination. She shook her head. 'No, he didn't.'

'I'm glad.' Evie wiped her eyes.

The sailor sprang forward to offer her a handkerchief.

'Why should I have hurt Larry?' Evie regained her composure.

'Because he toyed with your affection, he lied to you, and then he cast you aside.' Frances squirmed as she heard herself utter these blunt words.

'He didn't lie to me.'

'You knew he was engaged to be married?'

'No. of course not. But there was never anything going on.'

What? That was not what everybody said. 'Tell me everything,' Frances said.

The affair that wasn't an affair seemed innocent enough, starting with a few dance lessons. 'Ship life gets boring after a while, and you search for things to do,' Evie said. 'That's partly why we also give lessons in addition to doing shows and dancing with passengers in the evenings.' Larry had seized the chance to improve his skills.

'He wanted to learn all the latest moves,' Evie said, with a faraway, dreamy gaze. 'Foxtrot, and the Lindy Hop. He didn't really need lessons, lovely light on his feet as he was but he took them all the same. Every afternoon we'd dance for an hour, and then we'd chat. All harmless stuff.'

'And then his future wife and mother-in-law came on board.' Frances put her hand on Evie's. 'You'd fallen in love with him, hadn't you?'

'We had both fallen in love.'

'But it had no future.'

Evie's face puckered. 'How could it? A gentleman from one of the best families, and a penniless entertainer with no family tree to speak of?'

'Still, it must have hurt when he ended your friendship.'

'He didn't. He was a real gentleman, and kind and thoughtful.' Evie goggled at Frances. 'He wanted to marry me. He was going to tell Rosalie.'

That stopped Frances cold. 'You were going to get married?'

'No. I told him, no. It was a beautiful dream and impossible. He'd have regretted his choice soon enough when the people he cared about would have given me the cold shoulder. How could I do that to him?'

'Poor Rosalie. Marrying someone who secretly doesn't love you must be awful.'

'I don't think she ever loved him,' Evie said, in a worldwise tone. 'It was one of those arranged relationships where the families both agreed it would be a great match, and he'd felt sorry for her when she lost her father. Anyway, he told me it would be rotten to marry her when he was crazy for me. He always tried to do the right thing.'

Frances's hope soared as the meaning of these words sank in. 'If you weren't dead set on marrying Larry Vaughan, you had no reason to be jealous enough to kill him rather than see him with someone else.'

'Kill him? I loved him. I'd have done anything to see him happy.'

'Someone else did not love him. Do you have your cigarette case?'

'What?' Evie's forehead crinkled. 'I don't think so. I hardly ever smoke.'

'A similar case was found under Larry's bed. The shop originally had three of them, and they were all sold.'

'It should be in my evening bag,' Evie said. 'Larry gave it to me.'

'The bag is in your cabin?'

'It should be.'

The sailor tapped on his watch. 'Time's up, Miss.'

'One minute,' Frances said. 'Do you have any clue if there was bad blood between Larry and anyone else?'

'Everybody liked him. Although he wasn't too keen on Major Forsythe, and on that dreadful man they call Stinker for a good reason. Loathsome leech.'

'I can imagine. Don't despair, Evie. I'll see if I'm allowed to come back,' Frances said. 'One more question, why did Ada and Nancy think you hadn't given Larry the push?'

'That's what I let them believe because I didn't want any gossip. The least said, the soonest mended.'

'True.'

CHAPTER EIGHTEEN

'I'm so sorry, madam,' the shop assistant said when Mildred and Uncle Sal entered the store. 'I've found the receipt, but it doesn't give a name or a cabin number for the buyer. There were a few other items sold together with the cigarette case.'

'Other items? For a female, or a man?'

The shop assistant pursed her painted lips. 'A crystal fan hair comb and a silver flask.'

Aunt Mildred harrumphed. 'Not very conclusive. Your colleague really doesn't remember? Do you often have customers making several purchases?'

'Oh, no. One of the cabin boys brought a letter detailing the order, and he also paid in cash.'

'Do you have the boy's name?'

'I'm afraid we don't see them enough to know them.'

'Of course not. You've been most kind.'

The shop bell tinkled. Mrs Halsall, dressed from head to toe in smart black satin, rushed in.

'Hello, Mildred.' The other woman gave her a wan

smile. 'Do you mind if I jump the queue? I can't bear to leave Rosalie alone for more than a few moments. The dear child is heartbroken.' She dabbed her eyes with a lace-edged handkerchief.

'I'll come back later,' Aunt Mildred said to the shop assistant. 'I've decided on the golden cigarette case, and the vanity.'

'I'll have everything ready.' The shop assistant's dimples appeared again, making Uncle Sal wonder if the girl worked partly on commission.

'What can you show me in jet jewellery?' Mrs Halsall stuffed her handkerchief into her clutch. 'It doesn't feel right to wear diamonds and pearls when one has suffered the cruellest loss of all.'

Uncle Sal snorted, turning it into a cough to cover his callousness as his companion gave him a swift kick.

'That was not very gentlemanly,' she chided him as soon as they were out the door.

'I didn't mean to be rude,' he said. 'She just reminded me of an actress in one of the second-rate melodramas. '

'Not the lead role, I assume?'

'Gosh, no, more of a walk-on. Mind you, compared to your chum she was a proper Sarah Bernhardt.'

Aunt Mildred chuckled.

'What next?' he asked.

'An early afternoon tea for us, and then we'll return when the crowd is thinning.' Fair enough, people were out in full force, although Uncle Sal wondered what they hoped to discover in the arcade. The shops sold the same things as they had all along, with no new deliveries possible until they reached shore.

'Spoken like a frugal man of reason,' Aunt Mildred said as he mentioned his puzzlement. 'But let me tell you, spending hours in a beauty salon and the agonising over a new dress to show off your glossy curls or, in the case of gentlemen, to order a new shirt or two is simply one of those things one does in our circle. And since there's not much more to do than search for entertainment to fill the days and evenings, these stores will never lack for custom.'

She selected a spot on the observation deck for their afternoon tea. Their server placed the teapot and a three-tiered stand with finger sandwiches and small tarts on a table before he changed their deck chair setting to upright.

'Would sir and madam like a cushion, or a blanket?' His face showed well-mannered blankness.

'Both, please,' Mildred said.

'This is the life,' Uncle Sal said when they were alone. The next occupied deck chair stood three yards from them, and the tennis and shuffleboard players on the end of the deck created enough noise to cover up their conversation.

'If it wasn't for the tragic fact that a man is dead, I'd say this is the most diverting journey I've ever had.' She selected a salmon sandwich.

'It is fun to play the sleuth.' He helped himself to a morsel of lemon drizzle cake.

'Your friend Jack is a dab hand at this game, isn't he?'

'We've had a wee bit of experience with this kind of thing.'

She raised her plucked eyebrows. 'With murder, or with card-sharps?'

'Both,' he admitted. 'Once all this is over, there's a few tales we've got to tell you. Only –'

'Yes?'

'It's a lark to play all the different roles and ferret out information, but it can be a dangerous game. If a killer twigs you're on to him, they don't usually roll over and play dead, if you forgive me the pun,'

'Nonsense.' She nibbled her sandwich. 'It's sweet of you to worry but perfectly unnecessary. I can't imagine any danger befalling me.'

'But you do believe the killer is somewhere out here, among us? If it's Forsythe, I bet my last penny he won't go down without a fight. The same goes for Callaghan.'

'There is no doubt our man is still on the loose. But I wouldn't overrate his intelligence.'

'He did set up that poor girl as a scapegoat pretty well.'

'Really?' She wiped her fingers and picked a ginger nut. 'I'd have found it more convincing to stick to less evidence. The feather would have been ample to raise suspicion, but feathers, fabric, and a cigarette case? All that was missing was the glass slipper our Cinderella lost when she fled the scene of the crime.'

∽

Jack had used the same argument in his conversation with the captain and Mr Whalan. As happy as the ship's master would have been to wash his hands of the whole affair and hand Evie Miles over to the British authorities in Bombay, his conscience forced him to agree with Jack.

'The question is, what can we do?' His mouth set in a grim line as he stalked around his office with wide, angry steps. 'We have nothing to go on.'

'Has your doctor established the cause of death?'

'Devilish, that's what I call it. There was a whisky glass with a greyish sediment on the bottom from a sleeping powder. If you'd care to hear it from Doc Gifford himself, he'll be with us shortly, after his surgery hour.'

Jack had secretly wondered why one hour in the morning and one in the afternoon was considered sufficient for a ship with several hundred passengers and a couple of hundred crew from the engine room to the kitchen hands, but changed his mind soon enough when he overheard an elderly couple comparing imagined ailments as if it was a highly prized competition.

Dr Gifford made a good first impression on Jack. He had the looks of a matinee idol, with the first shots of grey spangling his brown hair, and a firm handshake that inspired trust.

To his commendation, he cut to the chase without wondering what Jack had to do with the investigation.

'There's no doubt the victim was poisoned,' he said. 'Vaughan must have managed to deposit his cigar in the ashtray before he lost consciousness, either from the spiked whisky or from the arsenic he'd been sucking on. The cigar butt was covered in the stuff. You could see the discolouration from the liquid.'

'Liquid? It had been soaked?' Jack pondered this fact.

'My best guess is, yes.'

'So, it would have had to dry again. Nobody would smoke a damp cigar.'

The doctor nodded his agreement.

'Have you made the experiment how long that would take? If we have any idea when the fatal cigar must have been smuggled into Larry Vaughan's cabin, we could find out where our suspects where during that hour or two.'

'I've got a cigar.' Captain Grey's tense shoulders relaxed. 'Now we're making progress.'

'Not too fast,' Mr Whalan said. 'What if he had a visitor who offered him a smoke? In that case there was no need to break in earlier.'

'The amount of ash should be able to tell us if there was only one cigar being smoked, or an additional cigarette.' Jack's neck prickled. He could feel they were on to something. 'What about the cigarette case?'

The captain stared at him without comprehension. 'What about it?'

'Have you had it tested for fingerprints? Who has touched it?'

'I discovered it,' Mr Whalan said. 'I put it in a box, together with the other clues.'

'Can you test it?' Jack rubbed his hands together. 'It'll be interesting to see what story it tells us.'

'With pleasure.' The captain unlocked a drawer and took out a small box with grey powder and an insufflator, together with the evidence box. 'I never thought I'd see the day when we'd have to use our detective kit. Show us what you've learned during your training, Mr Whalan.'

The First Officer used the insufflator to cover the cigarette case with a thin powder coat. He blew off any excess grains. The result under the doctor's magnifying glass, yielded a clear set of fingerprints.

Jack whistled. 'Beautiful. Do you have a photographic camera, or should I fetch mine?'

'I have one, in my cabin.' Mr Whalan hurried out of the door.

'I'll be darned if I understand why these prints make you so cheerful,' the captain said.

'Wait until your First Officer is back,' Jack said.

The doctor broke into a face-splitting grin. 'I've got it. I wouldn't want you on my tail should I ever stray from the path of righteousness.'

Mr Whalan returned. Jack asked him to take photographs of the fingerprints on the cigarette case and he obliged. The camera clicked away.

'And now, Captain, a sheet of your nice thick ship's paper and your ink pad for Mr Whalan, please.'

'Why?'

'Exclusion prints, right, Mr Sullivan?' The doctor slapped his thigh.

'That's correct, doctor. And it's Jack for you.'

Mr Whalan rolled his fingers one by one on the ink pad and pressed them onto the sheet of paper, leaving crisp imprints.

'What do you say, doctor?' Jack peered at the sheet.

The doctor compared the prints on the case and on the paper under his lens. 'Identical, no doubt. All the prints belong to our good Mr Whalan here.'

'Which means, the cigarette case was dropped on purpose. It was wiped off before, or it would have been covered in smudged prints.'

'Miss Miles had no reason to do that,' the captain said.

'No. But the murderer would.'

'I wonder. How much does a layman know about these details?'

'Quite a lot, I'd say.' The doctor pushed the sheet with the fingerprints over to Mr Whalan for more photographs. 'My mother reads every book of Agatha Christie's, and there's an excellent selection of mystery novels in our onboard library. The meaning of fingerprints and lipstick-smeared cigarette ends in detection are fast becoming common wisdom.' He smoothed his hair. 'If there's any role left for me in this investigation, I'm all yours, Jack.'

'How good are you at subterfuge?'

'I'm a decent poker player, if that's credential enough. Ask Mr Whalan.'

An idea formed in Jack's head. 'Do you play with passengers?'

'I could start.'

'We need to stop the rumours.' Jack addressed the captain. 'You're lucky your office hasn't been overrun yet by passengers demanding an explanation.'

'A few have cornered me already. I assure you I can handle them.'

'Mr Sullivan is right. We need an explanation, for Mr Vaughan's death and for Miss Miles' absence,' Mr Whalan said.

'The girl has a feverish cold,' the doctor suggested. 'And Vaughan died of an overdose of sleeping powders? I wish we could say heart attack, only it's not credible at all in a healthy young man.'

A vague memory stirred in Jack. A healthy young man in his regiment, a moderate drinker with a fondness for a cigar before he retired to bed. They'd found him one morning, cold and stiff, after downing a drink from a glass he'd fished a cigar butt out of. Everybody else would have done the same. Quality liquor was hard to come by on the frontlines, and during those few precious days on leave.

'Could he have died from nicotine poisoning? Nobody would expect you to perform a real post-mortem at sea.'

Dr Gifford pushed his lips back and forth, mulling over Jack's suggestion. 'He'd have to have steeped tobacco in his nightcap.'

'The cigar dropped in, he went to the bathroom and when he came back, he took out the cigar and finished his drink.'

'If he was half under, that'd be possible.'

'Wouldn't the sleeping powder explain why he wouldn't have reacted normally?' the captain asked.

'The question is, are we wise to his being drugged?'

Three pairs of eyes gave Jack a puzzled look.

'Was there a prescription found, or more powders, or a bottle that would explain the sleeping aid? If it wasn't his own on the other hand, that would have been risky. You can hide a lot of things from a lot of people. The person who cleans up after you is not among them.'

Captain Grey steepled his fingers together. 'I hadn't thought of that. So, how do you suggest we handle things?'

'That's easy,' Jack said. 'Dr Gifford, you're officially a sleuth.'

CHAPTER NINETEEN

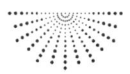

With three dress-maker shops on board, Aunt Mildred had allowed herself to be persuaded to let Frances tackle two of them. People gossiped, and they couldn't afford for the shop girls to wonder about Aunt Mildred's questions if she asked them everywhere.

Frances breezed into the first shop, named 'Mirabelle's'. Behind the counter stood a petite young woman who shifted her weight from one foot onto the other. Frances sympathised. Being on your feet all day was bad enough, but to stand in one spot hour after hour must be agony.

'Can I help you?' The girl stopped fidgeting.

Something about her stirred a memory. 'We've met before, haven't we? In the library reading room?' She'd wondered about the pretty young woman who always appeared engrossed in an Elinor Glyn novel without ever taking it out.

The shop girl blushed under her smart powder. 'We're allowed.'

'Gosh, I didn't mean any criticism.' Frances squirmed at the notion. 'It's simply that I hardly ever meet anyone else there.'

'It's wonderfully quiet,' the shop assistant agreed. 'Everywhere else on the ship is always crowded.'

Frances hadn't thought of that, but the only moments of real privacy she had she spent in her cabin, or in the library. Even during a moonlit stroll on the observation deck, one would bump into other people with the same idea. How much more crowded must it be for those crew members who couldn't freely mingle with the first-class passengers. But then, they might know each other better.

'I need a dress for our show,' Frances said. 'Something sparkly that'll catch the light. Like that mermaid costume I saw in the dancers' dressing room.'

'Are you one of the entertainers?' The girl's eyes shone bright with enthusiasm.

Frances had debated with herself if she should reveal her identity, but she saw no harm in it. If she admitted it to herself, she also basked in her little bit of glory. 'I'm assisting Salvatore the Magnificent,' she said.

'He's supposed to be ever so good.'

'He is, and more. You should watch us,' Frances said.

The girl pulled a disappointed grimace. 'We can't, unless we're invited.'

'What a pity. Do you have anything like that dress, or a similar fabric?'

'Let me see.' She disappeared behind a curtain. When she returned, she staggered under the weight of three bolts of fabric. Two shimmered like the ocean when they caught the light but the silk itself was unadorned. The third one matched the mermaid costume with its colours and the sequins.

Frances let the fabric glide through her fingers. 'It's a beaut.'

'It is, but you might want to consider. If you lose a few sequins, it won't look as good as the other fabric. And you might run into someone wearing a similar dress.'

'The mermaid dress is only used for the costume balls, so that shouldn't be a worry.'

'I sold a few yards of that fabric last week.' The shop assistant frowned. 'That is strange. Usually, the ladies have their dresses made up from us as well. We've got two seamstresses. But not in this case.'

Frances's heartbeat so hard against her ribs, she wondered if the girl could hear it. 'The customer bought only the fabric?'

'If it was her. There was a lady looking at it, but she didn't purchase so much as a button. Only, the next day a boy came with a written order and the money.'

'Do you remember the boy or the customer?'

The girl gave her a puzzled frown.

'I thought I could ask her what she plans to do with the fabric.' That excuse sounded flimsy even in Frances's own ears.

'I wish I could help you. All I can tell you is that she wore a black hat with a dark veil, and a white dress with white gloves. One of them had a tiny stain, but I didn't want to mention it.'

'Thank you,' Frances said. 'What's your name?'

'Dotty,' the girl said.

Frances proffered her hand. 'Thanks. Hopefully I'll see you in the library.'

∽

Two shops away, Aunt Mildred inspected scarves while the shop assistant served another passenger. Uncle Sal sat in a corner, holding her gift-wrapped parcel with the cigarette case and the vanity case.

She enjoyed the feeling of silk and velvet under her fingers, and the concocting of clever ideas. Only her kind heart prevented her from praying their investigation might last until they docked in England. The notion to exchange her exhilarating ship company for the utter predictability of her London life was too sobering to contemplate.

She admired one particularly ravishing headscarf in shades of reds and orange that might serve her well in an open car, as the other customers left. She beckoned the shop assistant.

'I wonder if you could help me,' she said.

'What can I do for madam?'

Aunt Mildred lowered her voice, a gesture she had discovered with success to inspire confidence. 'It's about the final masquerade ball.'

'Yes?'

'I want to make sure our costumes will not be duplicated. Do you have ready-made dresses?'

'Only if they're really popular and easy to adjust. Otherwise we recommend them made to order.'

'So, if I were to decide on a design, and another customer has a similar idea?'

'We'd check our order books to make sure it won't be exactly the same.'

'But it could be very similar at first glance?'

'We try very hard. Did madam have anything in mind?'

'Neptune,' Aunt Mildred said.

In the background, Uncle Sal groaned.

'For my nephew. In which case I would dress up as a mermaid.'

The girl kept quiet for a moment, probably letting the image sink in.

'Unless there are already mermaids and Neptunes out there. Or anything in the fabric you'd use to make my outfit. I was thinking of blue, and green, and sequins to resemble the scales on the bottom of the dress.'

A frown was the answer as the girl consulted a ledger.

'We did have an enquiry,' she said. 'A lady. I think she wanted to make sure we had something suitable before the gentleman she asked for would come and buy the wrong thing. It happens a lot, that we receive a hint, so to speak, where to steer our customers.'

'He wanted to buy costumes?' Mildred's pulse accelerated.

'Just fabric, for a stole.'

'Could you show it to me?'

The shop assistant fetched a huge sample book. It contained swatches of material in all the colours of the rainbow, including two that almost matched the mermaid dress.

'What a beautiful selection,' Aunt Mildred said. 'What did the gentleman decide upon?'

'He didn't come after all.' She giggled. 'Sometimes the

gentlemen get cold feet to come in here, if it's not for a wife or close relative, if you understand what I mean.'

'And the lady didn't seem to be one of those?'

'Hard to tell. She had her hat veil drawn all the way down to her chin.'

Aunt Mildred turned to Uncle Sal. 'What do you say, would my nephew enjoy being Neptune?'

'Why don't I sound him out and then you can decide?' Uncle Sal suggested.

'That does appear to be the best course of action,' she said and picked up the ravishing headscarf. 'For now, I'll have this.'

'Beautiful choice. It's one of our loveliest pieces,' the shop assistant said. 'Should I gift wrap it?'

~

Frances met up with them in the piano bar. With only half an hour left before dinner, most passengers were still changing into their evening wear or having an aperitif at their dining tables.

She couldn't wipe her grin off her face, and Aunt Mildred's expression resembled hers.

'You go first,' she said.

'There was someone trying to find the material in question on behalf of a man.' Aunt Mildred fell silent as the waiter brought a sidecar for her and Uncle Sal and lemonade for Frances.

'The man we're thinking of? The older one?'

'Possibly. I've seen no evidence that the other one had much to do with women, apart from ogling the entertainers. He didn't come to make the purchase. I assume, because it wasn't a perfect match. The woman wore a veiled hat, so we have no clue as to her identity.'

'But we do know she found what the man was searching for.' Frances took a refreshing swig. 'She visited "Mirabelle's", too. Dotty, the girl who works there, told me about the hat. And she sold the right fabric.'

'To whom?' Uncle Sal leaned forward, all ear.

'To whoever sent a boy with a written order and money.'

'The same story as with the cigarette case.' Aunt Mildred narrowed her eyes.

Frances nodded. 'Our mystery man went to a lot of trouble to keep his identity secret while collecting evidence to plant.'

'If it's the man in question, it shouldn't be too hard to find out which ladies he's friendly with. You've spent weeks in his company, Mildred. Is there anyone you can think of?'

She took a sip. 'He did share a table with the Halsalls a few nights, if I recollect correctly, and then of course there are the merry widows.'

'Who?' Frances asked.

'A group of ladies with one husband in the grave and a keen eye for the next one.' Aunt Mildred wrinkled her nose. 'Two or three of them were hanging on his every word, about his exploits in India. You'd have thought he was the Viceroy in person, the way he puffed himself up.'

'If only we could figure out who the errand boy was,' Frances said.

'We can't ask around, and neither can the captain,' Jack said when they had a quiet moment after dinner. 'We thought about it, but the bush telegraph on a ship is faster than lightning. Even if we had a name, it wouldn't be proper evidence.'

Frances grimaced. 'It's awful to think that that vile man is enjoying himself while Evie is sitting in that cabin, half scared to death.' Another thought hit her. 'That pickpocket you caught would be on the lookout for rich pickings, right? Do you think he ever emptied the major's pockets?'

'That's possible. Why?'

'If he has evidence that the man is cheating at gambling, the captain might authorise a cabin search.' Frances spotted Nancy in a mirror. 'I'll be back in a few minutes,' she said.

'Take your time.' Jack touched her back. 'Sal, Tommy and I will play a hand of cards or two with a new friend.'

'What about me?'

'Listen to an announcement Mr Whalan will shortly make before the dance is opened and see if anyone reacts weirdly.'

CHAPTER TWENTY

Subdued giggles from the dressing room told Frances that the other girls were preparing for their duties on stage or on the dance floor. She knocked and poked her head in.

'You're a godsend, Frances. Come on in and give us a hand,' Nancy said. She tugged at a zipper that was stuck halfway down Ada's back. 'It doesn't budge.'

Frances knelt to be in eye-height of the blasted thing. It had to be a figure-hugging silk dress too, with material so delicate any harsh treatment might rip it.

'We might have to open a few stitches,' she said.

Ada blanched. 'Good grief. Any damage will come out of our wages.'

'Then why did you squeeze yourself into this dress?' Nancy put her hands on her slim hips. 'Evie's the only one it properly fits.'

'But she's not here and it's the nicest dress by far.' Her friend pouted.

Silently, Frances agreed. The azure blue and the simple cut were divine.

'This might tickle,' she said as she slid one finger carefully between the frock and Ada's skin. She could feel where the zipper had caught on the lining. 'Can you suck in your tummy and hold your breath?'

'I'll try.' Ada groaned with the effort.

Frances inserted a second finger. A little wiggling, and the zipper came free. She pulled it down inch by inch, holding the lining pressed to the side.

'Maybe I should choose something else to wear.' Ada gave them a rueful chuckle as she climbed out of the frock.

'The silver one,' Frances suggested. 'It emphasises your blonde hair.'

'Smashing idea.' Ada effortlessly shimmied into the gown. 'Now, what can we do for you?'

'Can you let me into your cabin? Only for a few moments?'

'I'll go with you,' Nancy said. 'Ada's trying to win back her beau.'

She linked arms with Frances.

The cramped cabin might nevertheless have been cheerful with its colourful embroidered kimonos on hooks. A bowl full of cosmetics stood on the dresser, kept in place by a small rail that ran the length of the furniture.

Stockings hung from a line over the wash bowl, and what Frances took to be family pictures decorated the wall. For a fleeting second, Frances felt the sting of homesickness, and guilt when she remembered how little she'd thought of her mum lately. She promised herself she'd add to her letter later tonight. Or tomorrow at the latest.

Two of the beds were made up in haste. The third, a top bunk, was immaculate.

'I wanted it to be nice when Evie comes back,' Nancy said unprompted. 'Now, what are you looking for?'

'Her evening bag.'

Nancy opened a small wardrobe. One side held a row of drawers and shelves, where the girls had piled up their blouses and sweaters. The bottom shelf held bags. Nancy held out a clutch.

Up close, the material had a few shiny patches where the faded black sateen had been refreshed with fabric paint. Its contents were meagre enough. A lipstick, a handkerchief, old dance cards with Larry Vaughan's name among others, and a tin with breath mints.

'Where's the cigarette case?' Frances took out the items one by one and felt the lining. Nothing there.

'Weird,' Nancy said. 'She always took it with here, because it was a present from you know who.'

'Did she smoke a lot?'

'Hardly ever. She didn't really care too much for the smell.' Nancy's forehead creased. 'Why do you want the case?'

Frances couldn't think of any pretend reason. 'It might help her if we find it.'

'Really?' Without hesitation, Nancy flung the remaining bags on her bed and opened all the drawers in the wardrobe. 'Maybe Ada bummed a fag and put the case in with her stuff.'

But they came up empty. A crumpled cigarette pack was all they could find, and Nancy claimed it as hers.

'Drat.' She jumped up. 'I really need to go. Do you want to stay?'

Frances shook her head. 'Don't tell Ada, okay? The fewer people have any idea that we're trying to help Evie, the better.'

Her friend mimed zipping her mouth. 'That's smart. I mean, I trust Ada, but she can be a bit chatty when she's had a tipple or two too many.'

They made it into the ball room with only seconds to spare before Mr Whalan stepped up to the microphone.

He hushed the music as Frances slipped into her spot next to Aunt Mildred. Nancy hurried backstage.

'Ladies and gentlemen.' Mr Whalan paused, a sombre expression on his handsome face. 'I'm sure you're aware that we have suffered a tragic loss. One of our passengers died in his sleep.'

Loud murmur around Frances greeted this announcement. She risked a glance from under her lowered lashes.

Mrs Halsall, who'd appeared on her own, stoically suppressed tears. Frances's heart went out to her. Even if her daughter's engagement hadn't been a love match, it must be terrible to lose someone you cared about in this manner.

Major Forsythe allowed himself a small smirk.

Mr Callaghan, Mr Brown, Mr Fitch and Mr Sanders showed stony faces. Given Mr Wodehouse's excellent insights into upper class British men, Frances took that for the maximum amount of grief they were prepared to show the world.

'We have waited to inform you until we could ascertain the cause of death,' the First Officer continued.

Was that a nervous flicker in Major Forsythe's eyes? Whatever it was, he rose and quietly made his way out.

'On his way to the gambling tables,' Aunt Mildred whispered into Frances's ear.

'The doctor has completed his examinations. You can all rest assured that there is no danger to any of you, and this has nothing to do with a case of cold that keeps two of our crew members in their berths.'

A handful of people gasped. Frances approved of the smooth way Evie's absence was covered by this statement without naming her.

Mr Whalan allowed himself a sad little smile that reminded Frances of Gary Cooper in "Morocco" as he continued. 'That is, no danger if you take a few precautions. The passenger in question died of acute nicotine poisoning. We implore you, if ever your cigarettes or cigars come into direct contact with your drinks, do not imbibe them at all cost.'

More gasps and excited murmur arose.

'Though these cases are exceedingly rare, Doctor Gifford has informed me that involuntary nicotine poisoning is an easily avoidable but real threat. But now let's think of more pleasant things.' He gave the conductor a sign. At the first beats of "I Want To Be Happy", Nancy and Ada tap danced out onto the stage, bright smiles in place and for all the world to see, as carefree as anyone in the room.

One passenger gave them an appreciative once-over as he reached for his cigars. His females companion slapped his hand. 'You will not touch those filthy things.'

Frances stifled a chortle. Even Mrs Halsall's lips twitched. Mr Sanders glowered at nobody in particular, but then Mr Whalan's explanation had put paid to all his suspicions against the major.

He and his friends rose from their table. Tommy gave her and Aunt Mildred a swift signal that he'd follow them.

'Come, my dear.' Aunt Mildred took her clutch.

'Where are we going?'

If Frances had hoped for excitement, she was out of luck. All they did do was take Tinkerbell for a stroll around the observation deck before they settled in the piano bar for a nightcap. Everywhere they went, people talked about Mr Whalan's dramatic announcement.

Aunt Mildred and Frances shared a satisfied grin. They hadn't heard a single word of doubt. Only the tobacco vendors wouldn't be too happy. Smoking was going to become wildly unpopular until people forgot.

CHAPTER TWENTY-ONE

'*E*vening, sir.' Merry gave Jack a well-practiced smile. The gambling tables were in demand tonight, Jack saw with satisfaction. A second steward, a lascar in his traditional turban and a pristine uniform, took care of refreshments and any demands the gentlemen might have. He also stuck close to the craps and card tables preferred by Major Forsythe.

Jack appreciated the idea. If the man was a crook, he might be on his guard if an additional British steward worked in a room habitually served by only one man. A lascar though would be instantly dismissed as unimportant by a man such as Forsythe, and probably most of the men playing at cards and craps. They were used to not really seeing natives, or most servants really, unless there was a good reason to do otherwise.

Uncle Sal waved at him. He'd spent the evening entertaining a group of elderly men seeking not so much entertainment in the form of mild gambling, but an escape from the dancing and their wives.

'Jack, my boy.' He signalled the steward for another drink.

'Make that two drinks,' Jack said. The amber liquid in his and Uncle Sal's glasses that resembled whisky, came from a special bottle reserved for them. They needed a clear head and substituting cold tea for booze was an old trick Jack used at the Top Note.

He sat at the card table next to Uncle Sal's. This way they could watch the whole room instead of glancing at each other.

Major Forsythe strode in and made a beeline for a card table. 'There you are, old friend,' a weather-beaten gentleman said as he joined him.

A sneering Sanders placed himself so he could watch the Major. Brown tried to move him to another sport, without success. Callaghan and Fitch flanked him. Tommy, who'd entered together with Doctor Gifford, hesitated. Jack gave him a tiny signal to sit with Sanders and his friends.

'May I join you?' Tommy asked.

'We already have a foursome for bridge, so you'd have to be the dummy in this rubber,' Brown said.

'That's rather good of you. In the meantime, can I get you anything to whet your whistle?'

'Brandy for me,' Sanders said. The others nodded.

'Coming right up.'

Tommy procured four brandies and a glass from Jack's bottle for himself from the lascar steward.

The major's table had by now attracted two more players and he demanded an unopened card deck.

Dr Gifford made his way towards Jack's table. 'Evening,

Doctor,' one of the men in Uncle Sal's company said. 'I hope you're not here on business.'

'Pure pleasure, I assure you. Care to join me in a hand or two?'

The man moved over to sit next to the doctor. 'Blackjack okay? Chicken stakes only.'

'Suits me.'

All the games were well underway, when Tommy tapped the doctor on the shoulder as he raked in his modest winnings.

'Yes?' Dr Gifford gave him a weary look. 'I'm not doing any consultations outside surgery hours, my good man.'

'Gosh, no.' Jack marvelled at the ease with which Tommy reverted to bumbling young man. 'I only wondered, that is, Mr Whalan said – and my great-uncle is fond of a snifter or two at night and his cigar ...' The sentence petered out.

'You were wondering if there's any risk he'll put himself in harm's way.'

Tommy loosened his bow tie. 'Well, one does, somehow.'

'What's all that about?' One of the gentlemen gaped at the doctor who heaved a dramatic sigh.

'May I have your attention please? It will only take a minute.'

The players laid their cards down. The major held his a little too long for Jack's taste, and his fingernail dug into one. Habit, he thought, or he intended to raise the stakes considerably later.

Marking cards from a new deck with nicks from fingernails was easier to pull off if you played with a secret partner, which meant they'd have to investigate everyone who played regularly with Forsythe.

'It's about Larry Vaughan,' Sanders interrupted. 'Poor devil.'

The doctor agreed. 'Poor devil indeed. Picture of health, and then he managed to poison himself with nicotine.'

Shocked cries rewarded the revelation. Jack watched the faces. Again, Forsythe's reaction took a little too long and his expression had a forced air, but then he must have arrived in his room after hearing Mr Whalan's announcement in the ball room. Unless he'd made an as yet unaccounted for detours, he'd already heard their false cover story.

'That's what the First Officer said.' Tommy swiped back a curl with a nervous hand movement. 'But one does wonder.'

'If what you're wondering about is helping your uncle into a better world, don't think about it. These things tend to come out in the end.' The doctor winked at Tommy in a humorous manner. 'And don't ask me for the recipe, in case anyone else here is also wondering about lucky accidents. Not that this was anything but a tragic one.'

'Gosh, no.' Tommy fumbled. 'I mean, I wouldn't dream – ' He gazed around, his mouth open in a picture of foolishness. It gave him a smashing opportunity to observe reactions.

The major shot him a calculating glance. Sanders pressed his lips together into a thin line. Brown took out his cigarette case and snapped it open. 'Put it away, man,' Fitch hissed.

The doctor returned his attention to the game. 'Shall I be the bank?'

Two hours passed without an incident. The major had a streak of bad luck, followed by a couple of passable hands at poker. When he switched to craps, he fared better, although not so much as to raise suspicion.

If Forsythe had a partner, either he'd stayed away tonight or his talents outmatched Jack's investigating skills.

Dr Gifford raked in yet another win as a boy came in and gave Jack a whispered message. 'Mr Whalan asks for your company, sir.'

He smiled at his companions. 'That's it for me, I'm afraid.'

'Is anything wrong, my boy?' Uncle Sal's brow creased.

'Nothing to worry about.' He hesitated.

'Plenty of time for entertainment ahead.' Uncle Sal fell in with Jack who raked his hair back with all five fingers, indicating a five-minute wait for the doctor. Tommy had to stay behind, and watch.

Mr Whalan awaited them in the doctor's surgery. A triumphant gleam in his eyes made Jack's heart sing. 'You were in luck with our pickpocket.'

'Let's say, he had a lot to tell me in exchange for a little lenience.' He cocked his ears. 'I'll tell you everything once the doctor is here. In the meantime, there should be an excellent brandy hiding in that cupboard.'

He filled four glasses as the doctor arrived and snatched the bottle from him. 'Serves me right to divulge to you where I keep the good stuff. You could have brought your own bottle.'

'I'll make it up to you, Doctor.' Mr Whalan lifted his

glass in a toast. 'To all of you. It was our lucky day when you chose to travel on our good ship, gentlemen.'

'The case is solved?' The doctor pouted like a small boy deprived of his big adventure before he sipped his brandy.

'Not yet, but we're close.'

The pickpocket had selected most of his victims well, Mr Whalan explained. 'They were all a bit boozed up, and some of them had just made the acquaintance of the major at the gambling tables. On the first night, they'd be good for at least fifty pound in wins. He'd help himself to a tenner or two, nothing too greedy, and move on.'

'Why didn't he target the major on his winning nights?' Uncle Sal asked. 'Forsythe must have been rolling in money.'

'He did, once. The major had just had a flaming row with someone and drowned his fury in a sea of whisky sour. Our bird saw his chance and lifted the wallet when he noticed something else in the major's pocket.' Mr Whalan paused. 'Have a guess.'

'Vaughan wasn't shot so it wouldn't have been a pistol,' the doctor said.

'Close enough. He had a stiletto knife.'

'That's serious stuff,' Jack said.

'That's what our bird thought. He toddled off as soon as he could and hid in his bed.'

'Does he have any idea who the major had the row with?' the doctor asked.

'None other than Larry Vaughan. And according to our star witness, it's a miracle the major didn't resort to murder there and then, the way he glared at Vaughan.'

'That's all wonderful, but how do we catch him? None of this is hard evidence,' Uncle Sal said.

'That's why we'll do a proper search of his cabin tomorrow, at lunch.' Mr Whalan stared at his empty glass. 'All this talking is dry work.'

The doctor poured him another brandy. 'I assume you're off duty.'

'My watch ended hours ago.' Mr Whalan smacked his lips. 'I don't expect to find anything out in the open, but if there's a locked drawer or suitcase, we have our captive who can take care of that.'

'You want to use the services of a criminal?' Uncle Sal snorted.

'If we have to. Do you have a better idea?'

'What about me, Salvatore the Magnificent? I might not be nimble-fingered enough to empty your pockets, but locks are nothing.'

'He's right,' Jack said. 'I've seen him in action.' He omitted to say what circumstances he referred to. They had all veered outside the law on that occasion, all for an excellent cause.

'Perfect,' the doctor said. 'I'd like to tag along.'

Mr Whalan paused. 'I'm not sure that's a good idea.'

'Why not? Unless you have someone better equipped to discover arsenic.'

'A smart man would have rid himself of the stuff,' the First Officer said.

'I wouldn't be so sure,' Jack said. 'What if he needed it again? We can't even be sure he stole rat poison from your store.'

'Fair enough.' Mr Whalan gave in. 'One more snifter and we'll call it a night. We need our sleep if tomorrow we want to catch a murderer.'

CHAPTER TWENTY-TWO

'The bathroom is yours.' Jack knocked on the door to Uncle Sal's bedroom. During his ablutions, the cabin boy must have been in, because a small parcel lay on the table.

Inside, Jack found a deck of cards and a note. 'The deck you were asking for. Our observer spotted nothing out of the ordinary apart from a few small jerks of the hand and the unobtrusive use of a fingernail.'

He shuffled the cards and ran his fingers over them. The deck was the one from the night before. Jack figured it would take a night or two to mark all the important cards. Sure enough, he found tiny grooves on the back of the aces, jokers, kings and queens, all in different parts of the cards. Enough to have an advantage over the other players and next to impossible to spot.

If another player demanded a new deck, the small jerks could be habit, indicating a few other tricks, like an ace up his sleeve.

He chuckled. A cabin search should be enough to condemn the man.

~

'Good morning.' Tommy's chipper greeting at the breakfast table made Tinkerbell yap.

'Shh, my darling.' Aunt Mildred stroked the dog's head. 'Lower your voice a little, Tommy.'

'Sorry.' If he tried to sound contrite, he failed in Frances's eyes.

At the table next to them, Mr Sanders and Mr Callaghan both flinched at the noise. Their two friends had not come to breakfast.

Jack took pity on them. He beckoned a steward and gave him a few quick instructions to make up a pitcher with tomato juice, raw egg and half a dozen spices.

'Is that for hangovers?' Frances asked.

'Tried and true.' He leant over to Mr Sanders. 'If you don't mind, I've sent for a remedy. Don't set your faith on hair of the dog, it only makes matters worse.'

Mr Sanders nodded and winced.

'So, you're a good Samaritan,' Callaghan said with a smirk, his first encounter with Jack obviously not forgotten.

'Let's say, I've had my share of experience with your condition.'

Jack returned his attention to his own company. They finished their meal in silence.

'It's a miracle those two could stand upright after all their boozing,' Tommy said as they assembled in their suite. 'I couldn't quite make out if they celebrated our ruse that Larry Vaughan wasn't murdered after all or commiserated that the major wouldn't swing for it.'

'I wonder if Forsythe was working alone,' Uncle Sal said. 'Most card sharps I've met prefer to work in pairs. Easier to lure in the marks and fleece them.'

'I've been thinking along the same lines,' Jack agreed. 'I've asked Mr Whalan to contact the shipping agent's office, to see if there are some passengers that travel on the same ship as the major.'

'They could be usually working on shore and this is simply a voyage to new hunting grounds,' Frances said, warming to the theme.

'Clever girl,' Jack said. 'That's why Mr Whalan will also radio the police in India. If Forsythe has really lived there for years, he might be under suspicion.'

'Then our part is done?' Aunt Mildred's shoulder sagged before she rallied. Frances had to admit that playing detective could be exciting. She said, 'I don't think so. It would be good to find the woman who arranged for the purchases in the shops. Maybe she's the partner?'

Seeing the doubtful reactions, Frances added, 'Are you telling me it's men only at the gambling tables? And a woman would be especially useful, because nobody would think of her as cunning enough to be a professional con artist or work with one.'

'Frances is right.' Aunt Mildred jutted out her chin. 'We owe it to ourselves, and possibly to that woman, if she's only a, a -' At a loss for a word she turned to Uncle Sal.

'A patsy,' he said.

'That's right, a patsy.'

'But how do you plan to find out?' Tommy's brows knitted.

She patted his hand. 'I have my ways, dear boy. Don't worry about me.' That was all they could get out of her before she dismissed the men.

'Are you free or do you have another rehearsal?' she asked Frances once the door had closed behind them.

'I'm all yours.'

'Good. Meet me in the piano bar in an hour. Dress like my poor relative.'

Frances thought it wiser not to be offended. If she was honest, poor relative would sum her up nicely compared to Aunt Mildred.

∽

The piano tinkled in the background as Frances met up with Aunt Mildred. 'My dear child.' Two air kisses were planted next to her cheeks before Aunt Mildred led Frances to a cosy nook at the back of the half-filled room. A wall lamp gave off a golden glow, and a sugar pot and a lemon squeezer stood on the table.

The nook next to them was taken up by a group of middle-aged women Frances recognised as the ones her companion had named the merry widows. To her surprise, a bottle of champagne in front of them was three quarters empty, and that before lunch. Frances shuddered. No wonder the merry widows only appeared on rare occasions for the midday meals.

Aunt Mildred gave her an eloquent shrug. 'I've ordered tea for us.'

A handsome young waiter who caused the merry widows to titter, served them with a pot of fragrant Ceylon tea and an assortment of biscuits. He took the titter in his stride.

Aunt Mildred raised her voice in a stage whisper loud enough to be audible to the other women. 'A word to the wise, my dear, from someone much older than you. Most men are simply useless when it comes to shopping for gifts. Unless you want to end up with all kinds of hideous things and forever have to feign gratitude, so you won't hurt their feelings, men have to be taken in hand. Don't wait too long.'

'But how do you do that? My brother's been giving his wife bath soaps for the last three years.' Frances crossed her fingers behind her back as she lied. Her lovely brother had great taste and enough good sense to ask his wife what she wanted.

Aunt Mildred clucked her tongue. 'He's not a military man, I hope? They're the worst cases. It takes so much tact to avoid ruffling their feathers.'

She rose and walked over to the merry widows. 'Could I borrow your sugar?'

'Take the pot. We don't need it,' one of the merry widows said, a fortyish woman who'd be pretty if she relied more on nature and less on the artificial help from the beauty counter. 'I heard you're giving your young friend some advice.'

'It can't hurt to prepare girls for the pitfalls.' Aunt Mildred lowered her voice. 'I'm not talking about the obvious failings of men, of course. Not to someone newly engaged to be married.'

'Bring the girl over. The more, the merrier.'

Frances squeezed herself into a corner. Two of the merry widows merely giggled glassy-eyed and raised their glasses. The other one gave her a wide smile. 'So, I hear congratulations are in order.'

Frances blushed. 'Why, thank you.'

'But your friend is right. If you want a man to give you a present you have your heart set on, drop hints the size of houses. The poor darlings don't understand anything less.'

'I found it best with my late husband to visit the shops beforehand on my own and then either steer him there or make sure the sales assistant was well aware what she should show him. Although when they were stationed in Egypt, my friend's husband sent his batman to do the shopping, and of course he was nothing like the description the girl had. Instead of the most gorgeous lapis lazuli earrings, the poor woman received a set of cotton pillowcases.'

'That's men for you.' The merry widow inserted a cigarette into a holder. One of her friends lit it for her, after a little unfocused fumbling. 'It took me ten years of marriage to train my Walter.' Her eyes clouded over. 'And then I lost him to an accident.'

'I'm so sorry,' Frances said. 'But surely you must have other admirers? You're so beautiful.'

The merry widow took a deep drag and blew the smoke out through her nostrils. 'Thanks, darling. One does hope one hasn't lost one's charms. I don't want to become a lonely old spinster.'

'If I were you, I wouldn't worry about that,' Aunt Mildred said. 'Didn't I see that charming major paying you more than a little attention?'

The merry widow sighed. 'Among us girls, that's what I thought for a while. But then he stopped coming to the dances and instead spent his evenings with the other men, no doubt boring each other silly over politics and the cricket season.'

'But didn't you help him with his shopping? The sales assistant mentioned a lady with exquisite taste helping him.' Aunt Mildred remarked offhand. She sipped her tea.

The merry widow knocked over her glass. Frances picked it up for her. Luckily it had been empty.

'Major Forsythe? A woman?'

'It might have been another man. The description was very vague.' Aunt Mildred said. 'He beat me to a hair comb I fancied. Serves me right to dither.' She turned to Frances. 'Shall we freshen up before lunch?'

CHAPTER TWENTY-THREE

'That was a bust.' Aunt Mildred stomped her foot. 'I had so hoped we'd clinch the investigation before the men can beat us to it.'

'It must have been his secret partner, don't you think? Why would you wear a hat with a veil indoors on a hot day?' Frances asked.

'That only leaves us with several hundred suspects.'

'Not when you think about it. It would almost certainly have to be a lady travelling alone. Mr Whalan should be able to make a list.'

'And we could keep an eye on our man's interactions.' Aunt Mildred cheered up. 'Excellent notion.'

～

They were both too excited to be hungry, and in the dining room it would be harder to explain the absence of Jack and Uncle Sal. Instead, they nibbled a few sandwiches on the observation deck, wrapped up in warm blankets, despite the heating and the residual warmth of the sun hitting the glass roof. It was almost December.

Tommy played a vigorous tennis double with Mr Brown, Mr Fitch and Mr Sanders. Mr Callaghan had pleaded fatigue, although the hangover remedy Jack had sent over appeared to have done the trick.

Tink snuggled up to his mistress who fed him morsels of ham. 'I wish we could see what's happening.' Aunt Mildred wiped a few crumbs off her lap. 'If only everything goes to plan.'

A steward had been tasked with making sure Forsythe stayed in the dining room. If necessary, he had instructions to create an accident. Jack had estimated they'd need ten undisturbed minutes to search the cabin, because they could exclude the most obvious places.

Mr Whalan sent two lascars to block off the hallway under the pretext of scrubbing the walls. It would only take seconds to slip into the major's first-class cabin, but they could not afford to be seen. Rumours spread like wildfires in this closed shipboard community.

They slipped inside. The major had a taste for luxury he kept well hidden in public. There, he preferred well-cut but plain suits with a hint of the military. Here, he revelled in a padded silk robes and velvet slippers. A crystal and silver tantalus held two expensive bottles of scotch and gin.

'I'll take the bathroom,' Uncle Sal said as Jack stepped into the dressing room. Mr Whalan held watch by the door.

Jack patted down the dozen suits. The major had a fondness for heavy materials and deep pockets that could hold a dozen smaller items without looking bulky. In one he found a lighter and a case with two La Antiguedad cigars.

The trunk was covered in a silk lining. Jack checked it inch by inch for a secret compartment, with no luck.

He shoved the trunk back in its original position. A man like Forsythe would spot any difference and the cabin boy had no reason to disturb things in the dressing room. He opened a drawer. Bowties, stiff collars with high points, and an oversized jewellery case. Inside, a selection of solid gold cufflinks and a heavy signet ring inlaid with jet again spoke of more money than most military or ex-military men possessed.

Jack measured the depth of the case with his finger. It didn't add up. Somewhere inside must be a button or lever that would let him lift out the velvet-covered tray with the jewellery.

It was a tiny thing, hidden underneath the locking mechanism. Jack pressed it, and the tray rose. Inside the secret compartment lay a lethal looking stiletto knife and two small boxes with dice. Their manipulation was cleverly done. It took an expert to notice the difference.

'Found something,' he called out. Mr Whalan popped up in the doorframe and wiped his brow. 'Good.'

Uncle Sal joined them, a spring in his step. 'Shall we see who outdid the other?' He spotted the dice. 'Weighted?'

'Real craftsmanship, too. I'd say, Hong Kong or Shanghai. What do you have, the poison?'

'Wouldn't that be nice.' A metal contraption shot out of his sleeve, slender enough to be invisible, made to hold a card. 'I'd say someone definitely likes to have an extra ace up his sleeve.' He touched the knife. 'Or prefers a quiet means to end trouble.'

They spent another five minutes searching every nook and cranny but, in the end, they had to concede failure. While they had ample proof that the major's luck at the gambling table was something he actively helped along, his cabin held no trace of the poison that killed Larry Vaughan.

'What about the cigars?' Uncle Sal asked. 'Are they the same brand that the doctor found in the ashtray?'

'We'll have to ask him.'

∼

They strolled past the watchful lascars who at Mr Whalan's signal, packed in their scrubbing already spotless walls.

In the surgery, Dr Gifford was busy strapping up a sprained wrist, courtesy of an overenthusiastic shuffleboard player. He gave Mr Whalan a disappointed shrug as the First Officer poked his head through the door. 'Ten minutes,' he mouthed. 'Captain's office.' The doctor nodded as he tightened the bandage.

∼

'Let him run loose?' The captain thumped his desk as Jack made his suggestion to continue observing Forsythe. 'You said you found evidence in his quarters that shows he's a con man.'

'But we haven't actually caught him in the act.' Mr Whalan rubbed his chin. 'I believe Mr Sullivan is right. We have two days left until we make landfall. If I radio police and the governor's house, they can make enquiries. It's much better to handle the case without causing a great stir.'

'You just said, we don't have any proof. What if the officials in India and England don't have any either?'

'Don't you worry,' Jack said. 'There will be evidence enough to hand him over in Bombay.'

'How can you be so sure?'

A fraught pause ensued, until the doctor chuckled. 'I think you should just take Jack's word and not look a gift horse into the mouth.'

'What about the murder? It's one thing to get the man for cheating people out of money. Cold-blooded poisoning is a different matter. Prison is too good for the man.'

'There was nothing in his cabin,' Mr Whalan said. 'He's a smart customer. Unless we can pin him to the cigar that killed Lawrence Vaughan. The tobacconist swears he only smoked Perfectos from Lord's of England.'

'Which tallies with the butt I discovered. There's no sign that Forsythe ever visited him or bought anything but La Antiguedad cigars.'

A heartfelt groan was Captain Grey's only reply.

'If you can bring yourself to trust us a little longer, we'll come up with a plan,' Jack said.

'Do I have any choice? Mr Whalan, you are in charge of this operation. Don't disappoint me.'

∼

'We've been waiting for hours.' Aunt Mildred brought her pince-nez back into play, a sure sign she wasn't best pleased. The spoon clinked against the glass as she stirred her Mimosa. They had the small writing room off the library to themselves where she had had the foresight to have refreshments ready.

Frances stuck to orange juice, as did Tommy and Jack. Uncle Sal gratefully accepted a cocktail.

'We came as soon as we could,' Jack said. 'Why don't you start with telling us what you discovered?'

Frances snuggled into his arm as Aunt Mildred launched into her tale. She couldn't have wished for a more receptive audience. In return, she rewarded Uncle Sal with rapt attention as he recounted the men's exploits. Her heart went out to him for the way he gave Jack most of the credit, despite his natural inclination to enjoy the spot centre-stage.

Aunt Mildred reached for the champagne to top up her Mimosa. 'Does that mean we're out of avenues to pursue? All we have are bits and pieces that any lawyer worth his salt will tear to shreds.'

'Look at them,' Tommy said. 'They have something up their sleeves.' Frances giggled at his pun and he winked at her.

He did have a nice sense of humour and a lot of common sense when he decided against playing the quintessential, mildly stupid gentleman right out of the pages of one of Mr Wodehouse novels. His aunt must share Frances's sentiments, because she said, 'I'm so glad you've decided against sounding like a member of the Drones' club for once. Just don't make a habit of it, or you'll not make it far in the ranks of the Foreign Office. Overtly demonstrated intelligence tends to be frowned upon.'

'Oh, I say, Aunt Mildred, old girl. I mean, really.' He winked again, this time letting them all in on the joke.

'So, what are we going to do?' Frances asked. It was almost afternoon tea-time, and her stomach reminded her of her frugal lunch.

'I have the germ of an idea,' Jack said. 'Give me a few hours, and I'll hopefully be able to tell you all more after your show.'

Drat. She and Uncle Sal had all but forgotten they were scheduled to perform tonight.

A rap on the door made Frances start. What if somebody had overheard them?

She heaved a breath of relief as Merry entered, holding a silver tray with the most heavenly smelling mince pies Frances could remember.

'Enjoy,' he said. 'There will be quite a rush on them.'

'But it's not even December,' Frances said.

'We do like to get early into the festive spirit.' He twinkled at her. 'You're in for a treat. Tomorrow we'll put up the Christmas tree, ready for the first advent Sunday, and all the passengers are invited to help with the decorating.'

'We trim the tree?' She squealed in delight.

'Everyone?' Jack's slow smile sent a jolt of excitement through Frances. She knew that expression, and tone. He'd sussed out the last piece they needed to solve the puzzle.

CHAPTER TWENTY-FOUR

It took all of Frances's patience to wait until Jack was ready to reveal his plan. In the meantime, she occupied herself with writing to Mum. She filled the first page with descriptions of the food and the fashions and how much fun she and Uncle Sal had. At that point, the inspiration ran out. She didn't intend to lie to her mother, and unless she made things up there simply wasn't anything left to tell that had nothing to do with murder and other disagreeable topics.

If only the shop assistants had noticed more. That reminded her of something she'd almost forgotten.

She went in search of Aunt Mildred and Tommy. If Dotty was only allowed to watch their show if a passenger invited her, those two were the right ones to do it.

'Franny?'

Frances dropped her lipstick.

'I didn't mean to startle you.' Nancy peered at her in earnest concern.

'It's okay. I was miles away.'

'We could see that.' Ada smoothed her dress over her hips. 'I wish they wouldn't bring out those scrumptious mince pies. Two minutes in my mouth and forever on my hips.'

'In that case you shouldn't stuff half a dozen in your purse,' Nancy said. 'That's greedy.'

'It wasn't half a dozen and they weren't for me.' Ada fiddled with her hair. 'I asked Mr Whalan if he could get them to Evie.'

'Mr Whalan?' Nancy's mouth fell open.

'He's much more understanding than Mr Mackie. He promised she'll have those mince pies, and that everything would be fine.'

'He said that?' A rush of heat crept up Frances's throat. It was nice to reassure Ada, but she wished he hadn't done it. It only needed a few words in the wrong ears to spoil whatever trap Jack planned.

'He also made me promise to stick to the version that Evie's bedridden with a bad cold.'

'That's good,' Frances said.

'Yeah, that's what I thought. All the poor lamb has left now is her reputation.'

'I'm sure it'll be fine.' Nancy's troubled gaze made Frances's conscience sting.

'Do you really think so?'

'Sure it will,' Ada said. She leant closer to Frances. 'Pout,' she commanded.

Frances complied.

Ada twisted a facial tissue into a screw and rubbed off a tiny lipstick smear. 'That's better,' she said. 'Break a leg.'

'Are you dancing before we go on stage?'

'Not tonight,' Nancy said. 'We'll be watching you from the bar. Our dance partners have invited us.' She pulled a resigned face. 'I swear, they make us earn every single penny.'

After one last lingering glance into the mirror, Ada tore herself away, taking Nancy with her.

Inwardly, those girls must be worried sick, she thought. Ada acted so tough, and yet it took only one wrong accusation to destroy them.

If only Jack's plan worked, whatever it was. The alternative didn't bear thinking about.

It took all her will power to concentrate on their routines, and if her bright smile faded once in a while, she couldn't help it. Still, for the first time in Signorina Francesca's life, she couldn't wait to leave the stage.

'You were smashing.' Dotty clapped her hands as Frances and Uncle Sal made their way to their table. 'No wonder people think you're both the bee's knees.'

'I'm glad you enjoyed it.' Uncle Sal kissed Dotty's hand.

'It's the best night I've had in weeks.' She gawked as she soaked up the elegant surroundings, and the crowd in their evening finery. Something caught her attention.

She whispered to Frances, 'Who's that lady over there, at the bar?'

Frances craned her neck. 'That's Rosalie Halsall,' she said. 'I didn't expect to see her tonight with her mother. Why?'

'See that small dark stain on her left glove? I could

swear it's exactly like the one the mystery woman in my shop wore.'

Frances and Aunt Mildred shared an excited glance. Rosalie Halsall had no reason to wish her fiancé harm, unless she hid an insane jealousy under her detached demeanour. But Frances could easily imagine her going along with any scheme that might destroy Evie's reputation, or just to play a prank on her rival.

She needed to tell Jack, who at this moment had gone to order a light dinner for her and Uncle Sal.

'Is anything wrong?' Dotty asked.

'Champagne?' Tommy asked, before Frances could come up with an answer.

'Only one glass,' Dotty said. 'I can't afford to get tipsy and make a fool of myself.'

'A wise decision.' Aunt Mildred pointed at her glass too. 'I'm so glad you could follow our invitation.'

'It's been ever so nice of you,' she said. 'I mean, we do get asked, only it's mostly ...' She chewed her lip.

'Someone you'd rather not invite you?' Uncle Sal guessed.

Dotty shrugged. 'I can understand people getting bored if they've nothing to do all day. And if you're a man travelling alone – and we're allowed to say no. Actually, we're supposed to say no.'

'I'm glad to hear that. Would you like to dance?'

Dotty clung to Uncle Sal's arm as he led her to the floor and into a slow foxtrot.

At the stroke of midnight, Uncle Sal and Aunt Mildred dropped the delighted shop girl off outside her cabin and rushed back for a final discussion.

Tommy sprawled in his wing chair, courtesy of Tinkerbell who'd settled on his lap, with his head pressed against Tommy's chest.

'Well,' Aunt Mildred said. 'How are we going to trap our man?'

'I'll tell you as soon as our final visitor has arrived,' Jack said. 'I've asked Mr Whalan along. I hope you don't mind.'

'Fiddlesticks. He'll be useful. I have a high opinion of his mental faculties.'

Frances covered up a yawn. As much as she wanted to hear every detail of the plan, she couldn't help being tired.

Jack took her hand and gave it a tender squeeze. 'It's almost over, my love, and then you can relax.'

CHAPTER TWENTY-FIVE

Frances splashed her face with cold water to properly wake her up. Despite the simplicity of Jack's plan, it had taken them until two in the morning to work out the choreography. It all depended on having the key players close to each other for a few moments.

She needn't have worried. The doctor had charmed Mrs Halsall into telling him how her beautiful daughter, who once again skipped breakfast, coped after her brave appearance at last night's dance.

The dutiful mother blossomed under his soothing influence and let herself be led to a quiet corner, close to a spot where Aunt Mildred had monopolised the major with questions about the Raj and the importance of keeping up good British traditions throughout the empire.

Mr Brown lounged nearby, smoking a cigarillo.

Half hidden from their view by a column, the captain and Mr Whalan had what Frances knew to be a serious discussion.

She shamelessly eavesdropped with Jack, although to

an observer it would seem like two lovers engrossed in each other.

'That's not enough evidence to hang a dog on,' she heard Captain Grey say.

'You don't mean to say Mr Vaughan's death might go unpunished?'

'Not if I can help it, but as long as we don't find the poison ...'

By now, both Mrs Halsall who'd no doubt repeat everything to Rosalie, and the major both had a hard time to hide their interest in the conversation, Frances noticed with satisfaction.

'We've searched her quarters,' Mr Whalan said. 'And she can't have disposed of it in any of the public places because our staff would have found it. The open deck was locked, so she couldn't have thrown it overboard.'

'There's only one place left to search then.'

Frances hid a smile. Both men outdid themselves. Jack pretended to whisper sweet nothings into her ear.

'What do you mean?'

'There's one spot we haven't turned upside down, Mr Whalan. The victim's quarters. If we find the poison there, it'll be enough to convince any jury.'

'I'll do it straight away, sir.'

'At lunch time, when everyone is occupied. We can't have any busybodies poking their nose into our affairs.'

Jack and Frances strolled away, hand in hand. In two hours, morning tea would be served, when the next part of their ploy would be set in motion. Then they'd be sure if their ploy was successful. Only one actor still had his part to do.

To distract themselves while they waited, Frances and Jack entered into a shuffleboard game, while Uncle Sal and Aunt Mildred played chess, and Tommy took Tinkerbell for a walk.

As he approached them exactly two hours and fifteen minutes later, Merry patted his pockets. The key ring that had protruded only minutes before he served morning tea to Major Forsythe, Mr Callaghan and his friends as well as the Halsalls, had disappeared. He cleared his throat twice. Captain Jack answered with a curt nod. The bait had been taken.

CHAPTER TWENTY-SIX

The crowd oohed and aahed as the stewards carried in a ten-foot high pine tree. They'd cleared a space in the centre of the dining area and erected a dais for it. Two trunks full of Christmas ornaments and twinkling lights stood ready.

Frances's stomach tingled. Every single passenger had been promised one ornament to place so they all could join in the fun of decorating the tree. Boughs of holly decorated the stage. The tables each sported a sprig of it, with the berries glowing like rubies between the spiky dark green leaves.

Part of her brain wondered how long the plants would stay like this before they would lose their beauty, but mostly she marvelled at them. Not much longer and they'd be deep within the Northern Hemisphere, on their way to a British Christmas with ice and snow on cobbled lanes instead of scorching sunshine on baked red soil.

She glanced around under her lashes. Aunt Mildred stood at the front, together with Tommy and Uncle Sal.

Frances kept her place at the back, enjoying the vantage view it gave her.

Ada and Nancy kept their elderly dance partners company, and Mr Callaghan and his friends pressed their way forward.

Frances also thought she'd spotted Rosalie, but in that case, she had already cast off her mourning clothes and decided on a silver dress with sequin-studded shoulder straps.

Her mouth went dry as the Captain shook a bell and gave Mr Whalan a sign to open the trunks.

A woman squealed in delight as she picked a black and gold bauble. Mr Whalan slipped out of sight.

Frances remined herself to stay calm and concentrate on the tree and the crowd. Hopefully nobody had noticed Jack's absence.

~

Jack wiggled under the bed. He tried to roll onto his shoulder. It was just about doable, not ideal if he had to leave this spot in a hurry, but it would do. He knocked a tattoo on the wood above him. The bedspread was rearranged in precise folds.

It fell half an inch short, allowing him a glimpse of Mr Whalan's shoes as the First Officer took up his spot in the dressing room. He carried a pistol while Jack only had his hands and feet as weapons. He fervently hoped he wouldn't need them.

His nose tickled, He slowly pinched his nose until the urge stopped, all the while keeping an eye on the door.

∽

Aunt Mildred took her sweet time over selecting her ornament. She picked up baubles and stars, metallic birds with long tail feathers and checked them from every angle.

'Get a wiggle on,' a male voice shouted from behind. 'Some of us want to be done before nightfall.'

Aunt Mildred quelled the speaker with one regal glance through her pince-nez. She held a turquoise bird once again against the light and pinned it onto branch.

Uncle Sal added a matching bird, so they faced each other on the tree.

Frances tapped her foot in a nervous motion. Ten minutes had passed. How much longer until the first passengers would mill around again? The murderer would have to act fast or risk being spotted.

∽

The thin silk thread Jack had fastened to the door handle fell to the ground. The door cracked opened and barely audible steps moved closer to Jack's hiding-place. He breathed in and out as shallow as he could, to be unheard.

The steps moved away, towards the late Larry Vaughan's dressing room.

Jack could hear the door creak as the intruder entered that space. He lifted the bedspread an inch and risked a geek. The door to the dressing room was half closed again.

He rolled out from underneath the bed and squeezed against the wall, next to the door jamb.

"Stop,' Mr Whalan cried out.

Jack jumped into the door opening and blocked it with his body. With a furious cry, a woman tried to scratch him with her claws painted in blood red. Jack's hands caught her wrists and held them in an iron grip.

Mr Whalan took the vanity case she'd dropped and opened it. Next to powder, rouge and lipstick rested a small vial, labelled rat poison.

He said, 'Would you care to explain this, Mrs Halsall?'

∼

They escorted the woman to the captain's office. Jack went beside her, smiling as if everything was well with the world at the few passengers they encountered. Mr Whalan had shown his pistol to the prisoner, to remind her that there was no escape.

So far, she kept her icy silence. That was fine with Jack. The story only needed to be told once to Captain Grey, and again when they handed Mrs Halsall over to the police when they reached Bombay.

The captain flung the door open. Only a widening of his eyes betrayed his surprise as he saw who they'd caught.

Mrs Halsall bared her teeth at them in unmasked venom as the First Officer clapped handcuffs around her wrists and made her sit down on a hardbacked chair. The veneer of the society lady had disappeared completely.

Mr Whalan used his handkerchief to take the vial from the vanity case. 'I'd suggest you lock this away in your safe, Captain. Careful how you touch it. The police might be interested in fingerprints.'

'It doesn't even look like our bottles with rat poison,' Captain Grey said.

'It didn't have to. Would you have thought twice about comparing them had you found poison in your suspect's possession, or somewhere else she could reasonably have hidden it?' Jack leant against the wall.

'True. Why did you kill your future son-in-law, Mrs Halsall?' the captain asked.

She pressed her lips together until nothing, but a thin red gash remained.

'Why don't you ask her accomplice?' Jack suggested. 'Mr Whalan, would you be so kind as to fetch Rosalie Halsall?'

'Stop.' Two angry red spots appeared on her powdered cheeks. 'Leave my daughter alone.'

Captain Grey smirked. 'Mr Whalan, get the young lady, now.'

'She had nothing to do with it.' Mrs Halsall seethed with anger.

'So, you decided to murder your daughter's fiancé without her knowledge? That sounds a bit far-fetched. And why kill him at all? Breaking off her engagement with him would have been easier, don't you think, if she wanted to be rid of him?'

'Her breaking it off? The bastard was going to dump my darling, over that jumped up little creature.' Spittle formed in one corner of Mrs Halsall's mouth.

Revolting, thought Jack. 'Are we supposed to believe that?' he asked. 'Miss Miles had no intention at all of becoming Mrs Vaughan.'

'Lawrence didn't care. He thought if he ended his

engagement, he'd change her mind. Common little gold-digger. She was only playing hard to get. I've seen that type. Getting her claws into decent men and seducing them away from wife and home.' She broke into something resembling half sob, half hiccup. 'I told him, he could set her up in an apartment, see her discreetly, but no.'

'And that wouldn't have been seducing him away from home?' The captain recoiled in distaste.

She gazed at him in astonishment. 'Who cares what a man does at night, as long as he's back for breakfast and nobody is the wiser?'

'And the woman has the ring, and in due course, the title.' Jack felt sick.

'Every mother would understand that I couldn't stand idly by and see my daughter's reputation be destroyed.' Mrs Halsall's bosom heaved. 'My Rosalie would have been a laughing-stock, discarded for a cheap piece of skirt from the chorus. And don't tell me she had no intentions on him. I saw her one morning, just before the ball, sneaking towards her cramped little hole where she patently had not spent the night.'

'She'd stayed with a friend, a female one, because her roommates had accidentally locked the door.' Jack decided to keep this part of the conversation from Frances. The last thing he wanted was for her to feel bad about giving Evie shelter that night.

'Not enough that you murdered a man who trusted you, a man your own daughter cared about enough to accept his marriage proposal.' Mr Whalan said, revulsion openly written on his face. 'You also framed an innocent girl in cold blood. She might have spent the rest of her life in prison for your crime. Or worse.'

'Innocent? If she hadn't seduced Larry, none of this would have happened. I wanted her to pay for what she's done to us.'

She reminded Jack of a viper, cold blooded and full of venom.

'I expect you to write and sign a full confession, unless you want your daughter to be brought in as your accomplice.' Captain Grey opened his drawer and produced a stack of paper with the ship's letterhead, and an official stamp. 'Afterwards, lock her up, Mr Whalan. I'm glad when we can hand her over to the proper law enforcement.'

CHAPTER TWENTY-SEVEN

Jack came to the dining room just as the last ornaments were put up. He winked at Frances as he placed a star on a branch. The tree glittered and sparkled.

She gesticulated to Aunt Mildred, Uncle Sal and Tommy who hurried over.

'Can we congratulate you?' Aunt Mildred asked.

A slow grin spread over Jack's face as he pulled Frances into his arms. A happy sigh escaped her.

Aunt Mildred raised a finger. Merry appeared out of nowhere. No, not appeared. He shimmered into being, Frances thought in admiration for Mr Wodehouse's accurate descriptions in his novels.

'You may bring a bottle of champagne to my suite in ten minutes,' Aunt Mildred said. 'No, better make it two.' She sashayed off, expecting everyone to follow in her wake.

'We'll need another glass, Merriweather,' Aunt Mildred said as the steward served the champagne.

He cast a fleeting glance over the table and the five glasses he'd set out.

'Don't worry, you did not make a mistake,' she said. 'I'm expecting another visitor.'

Frances and Jack exchanged a surprised shrug.

Uncle Sal rubbed his hands with glee.

A hesitant knock on the door announced that person. 'If you'd be so good as to open, Merriweather?'

Mr Whalan strode in, with a slim figure in a hooded cloak by his side. He gave Aunt Mildred a quick nod. 'I'll be back in an hour,' he said and closed the door behind him.

Aunt Mildred beamed into the round. 'You 're all acquainted with my guest of honour. Tommy, wold you be so kind as to take Miss Miles's cloak.'

'Evie!' Frances grabbed her friend's hands and whirled her around. 'I'm so glad. But why is Mr Whalan coming back for you?' She half-turned to Jack. 'I thought everything is solved.'

'It is,' Jack said. 'But we've come up with a plan to protect both Evie and Rosalie Halsall's reputation. Once we've reached port, the police will arrest Mrs Halsall, and the embassy will take care of her daughter. Officially, they'll have left because of Mrs Halsall's health. When that's done, Evie will be officially applauded for assisting the captain with setting a trap for the murderer.'

'How's that going to protect Rosalie?' Frances sat on the sofa, saving the space next to her for Evie. 'Everybody on board will tell all their friends and family about the murder.'

'The captain will use a made-up name to satisfy curiosity, and we'll make sure people remember all the dark insinuations about cheating at cards and revenge. The rest is human nature.'

'Your idea, I take it?' Uncle Sal raised an imaginary hat to Jack.

'Mine and Mr Whalan's. The captain hasn't got the right kind of imagination for a little subterfuge.'

A small woof came from the bedroom. His owner rose. 'Tommy, you fill the glasses while I fetch Tinkerbell, and then I want to hear everything.'

Evie moved closer to Frances, as if needing her support.

As soon as Aunt Mildred let him go, Tink jumped onto the sofa and curled up on Evie's lap.

'Naughty Tinkerbell.' Aunt Mildred wagged a finger at the corgi and reached for him.

'I don't mind.' Evie fondled the silky ears. 'It's nice.'

Tommy blew out his breath. 'Can we please cut to the chase before the First Officer bundles Miss Miles away again?'

They listened wide-eyed as Jack reported.

'She must have decided to kill Larry the second she overheard his intentions to cry off his engagement,' Jack said.

Frances thought back to the conversation she'd overheard weeks ago, and the other unseen person. That must have been Mrs Halsall or her daughter.

'So, if he'd told Rosalie instead of me, he'd still be alive?' Evie shivered.

'Don't even think you're to blame in any way. She could rely on Larry doing the gentlemanly thing and talking to his fiancée in private. Then nobody but Rosalie and herself would ever know the truth.'

'But if Evie told someone else?' Frances asked. 'Then the story would have been out.'

'That wouldn't wash, not with the sort who mattered. If it's the word of a lady against a singer and dancer they'd never believe Miss Miles.' Tommy had the grace to colour.

'But to lessen the risk of a drunken confession to one of his mates, he had to die fast,' Jack said.

'The lost cabin key,' Frances said.

'She took it from his pocket when he was occupied. Their cabins were next to each other, and she was well acquainted with his nightly habits. Much better than Evie would have been. She doused his cigar in arsenic, dissolved a few of her sleeping powders in his whisky and let nature take its course.'

Despite the beastliness, Frances found herself fascinated by the puzzle. 'How could she be sure he'd smoke the right cigar?'

'She removed the rest from his humidor case. If he'd noticed, he'd have suspected his steward to have helped himself to the smokes.'

'Larry drank his nightcap as he enjoyed his cigar.' Uncle Sal rubbed his neck. 'So, he'd be too drugged to yell for help before the arsenic snuffed him out?'

'The cigar was found in the ashtray, only one quarter smoked.'

'I hope they lock her up and throw away the key forever,' Tommy said. 'What a rotten way to go, and to set up Miss Miles like that, why, it's the worst thing I've ever heard.'

Uncle Sal grimaced. 'Seems I owe you a tenner, my boy. Major Forsythe had nothing to do with it.'

Evie's eyes widened in surprise. 'But they introduced them to him. The major used to be chummy with Mrs Halsall. That's why Larry thought it'd all be above board with the gambling.'

Tommy's mouth fell open. 'That blackguard.'

Aunt Mildred appeared pensive. 'I remember there were a few rumours in London last year, about Doreen's expensive tastes and her husband's disapproval, just before he fell ill.'

'Stop it.' Evie trembled. 'This is too ghastly to think about.'

Frances chafed Evie's icy hands. 'You're right. What matters is that you're safe.'

'And that we finally finish that champagne,' Uncle Sal chimed in. 'We better make sure Captain Grey puts you up in his best cabin, young lady.'

'Would you mind sharing it with me, Frances?' Evie mastered a small smile. 'He said he has Merry prepare a suite, but I don't want to be there all alone.'

'What about Nancy and Ada?'

Evie wrinkled her nose. 'They'd only blab, and I'm supposed to stay hidden for a bit longer.'

'Then I'll be happy to keep you company,' Frances said.

'How very satisfying.' Aunt Mildred signalled Tommy to refill the glasses.

'And then you young folks should go and have some fun,' Uncle Sal said. 'Let the older generation catch our breath.'

He twinkled at Frances. A chuckle rose in her throat as she twigged his meaning.

~

Mr Whalan picked up Evie punctual as clockwork.

'Miss Palmer has agreed to share my new cabin, if that's okay,' the young woman said with a nervous flutter in her voice. She pulled the hood of her cloak deep into her face.

'I'll have the transfer of luggage arranged.' He smiled at the girls, looking more like a film star than ever.

'Can you give her friends the good oil?' Uncle Sal asked.

'The good what? Oh, you mean the news about her innocence. I'm afraid that'll have to wait a little longer.' Mr Whalan led Evie away.

Aunt Mildred put a hand on Uncle Sal's sleeve. 'You must teach me more of these delightful Australian phrases.'

'Too right I will. Why don't we start once the youngsters are out from under our feet?'

~

Tommy dragged his chain as they strolled towards the observation deck. 'I feel like a bit of a cad,' he said. 'What does one say in this situation when one runs into –' He ran his fingers through his slick hair.

'I wouldn't worry about that,' Jack said. 'I'd expect a cold or a similar excuse for the daughter to keep her to her cabin.'

'Gosh, I hope so.' Tommy 'Do you think the girl was in on the trick with the major?'

Frances had asked herself the same question. Rosalie was anything but stupid and should have had at least a good inkling what her mother was up to.

'I'd give her the benefit of the doubt,' Jack said. 'That is, unless you intend to marry into the family. In that case I'd strongly recommend you against it.'

'Heavens, no. But one does tend to run into each other constantly in London society.'

Jack patted Tommy's back. 'I wouldn't worry about that either. A prolonged stay in the colonies isn't only fashionable for young men who blotted their copy book.'

They entertained themselves the rest of the day playing shuffleboard. After dinner, Frances reluctantly excused herself. Evie had spent too many hours already imprisoned and scared. The least Frances could do was make sure she had company.

She'd borrowed a stack of novels and magazines from the library, and the discreet Merry had delivered them to her new cabin where he would now take her.

∽

Tommy slipped away, too.

Jack did the same. Uncle Sal and Aunt Mildred seemed to do fine without anyone else, Jack thought. His old friend was up to something. Good on him. Whatever it was put a spring in his step.

The first stars speckled the sky. Jack settled in a deck chair outside and selected a sheltered spot. He opened his neglected sketchbook. Mrs Halsall's face sprang unbidden to his mind, with her handsome features distorted by her own bile.

He pushed the image aside and picked up his pencil. Peace settled over him as a picture emerged on the page, of a small dog sniffing out Christmas ornaments. Tink, helping with the decorations. That would serve as a gift for their new friend.

'Sir? Would you like a blanket?'

Jack came back to the present. He hadn't noticed the chill in the air or the crick in his neck. 'No need,' he said to the steward. He didn't remember the man's name, so used was he to have Merry or the cabin boy Sam around. Silly really, on a ship this size.

He stashed the sketchbook in his pocket. The deck was almost deserted. Only a couple of hardy souls swaddled in coats and blankets braved the cold. Although they were still close to the equator, the night temperatures dropped in a blink, and the ship officers had exchanged their tropical uniforms of crisp white cotton for the traditional heavy navy-blue attire. In two days, they'd make land for the first time since they embarked in Adelaide, just in time for December and the start of the Christmas season.

He rolled his stiff shoulders and checked his watch. Not yet eleven. Having an early night would be a good idea.

Regretfully he decided against it. As much as he valued Tommy's good sense, he wouldn't be the first cove to say a wrong word when he'd had one over the eight.

The bars yielded no result. Jack pushed on, to the gambling room. Sure enough, Tommy sat a bridge table with three elderly gentlemen. In full view of him, Forsythe played craps with a young couple. Jack had only noticed them before because they drank too much and tipped too lavishly. Everything about them shouted new money, from her jewel-encrusted cigarette holder and diamond clips in her shingled hair to his oversized signet ring that failed to successfully hint at an heirloom.

At his card table, Sanders kept a beady eye on Forsythe, while his friends watched him with an air of good-natured resignation.

The situation tickled Jack's sense of humour. The only person who seemed oblivious to all this watching appeared to be Forsythe and the crap players. The young couple would be safe enough for a night or two while Forsythe whetted their appetite. The one thing that people forgot about weighted dice was that you could just as easily select to lose with them.

That's what Forsythe did now. The young man rolled the dice and hit the back stop. His wife jumped excitedly. 'Bonzer throw.' Her voice had a breathless quality. The dice rolled out to an eleven.

Forsythe threw his hands up in the air. 'I don't remember when I last saw someone as lucky as you, old chap. You've taken me to the cleaners, again.'

The young man puffed up his chest as he raked in twenty shillings.

Tommy's jaw tightened. Jack gave him a signal to go on playing bridge as he earwigged.

'I'm his lucky charm.' The wife purred at her spouse. 'Just you wait until we get to London.'

'Have you been to the old metropolis before?' Forsythe absent-mindedly pocketed the dice.

'My honey here was born in Southampton. The old

folks shipped out before he could walk.' She planted a resounding smack on his cheek.

He playfully slapped her bottom. 'Isn't she the cat's meow?'

'I'd be delighted to show you around.' Forsythe flashed his white teeth at them. 'Not many joints in good old London I don't know about. Your honeymoon, is it?'

'Too right it is. My parents have a farm back home, and we were up hard enough with the mortgage payments. Would you believe I was just rounding up sheep for crutching when I stumbled upon an opal this size?' He formed an o with his fingers. His wife snuggled up against his shoulder.

'Worth fifteen thousand pound,' she said. 'Just like that, we were rich.'

What a pity they couldn't purchase an ounce of good sense with the money, Jack thought. These two practically begged to be fleeced, by Forsythe, or another man of his ilk.

'I would never have taken you two for country-dwellers,' Forsythe said.

She simpered. 'You're a pet. We only went for a few days to help the old folks on the farm. My husband's in business and we're going to London for good.'

'You have to be careful who you're dealing with in the city. There's a lot of sharks hanging around, waiting for trusting people.' Mr Sanders flashed the young couple a trust-inviting smile that would have made his old public school proud. 'Sorry to intrude but I couldn't help but overhear.'

The young man tapped his nose. 'No flies on me, I'm telling you.'

'Nevertheless,' Mr Callaghan said. 'My uncle runs a small mercantile bank. I'd be happy to introduce you, and to a proper solicitor.'

'Aren't you sweet?' The wife batted her blackened eyelashes at him.

'One more word to the wise. Don't tell people how much you're worth. You wouldn't want to give anyone silly ideas.' Sanders' eyes glittered.

A muscle in Forsythe's jaw twitched as he gave a vigorous nod. 'Listen to the gentleman,' he said. 'Better safe than sorry is my motto, and that's what I always taught the young bucks in my regiment.'

The clock struck midnight. A steward rang a gong outside the door.

The wife snickered. 'They do keep strict bedtimes here.'

'It's the only way to clean up for the next day,' Forsythe said. 'Good discipline, that.' A quick clicking of his heels drove home his military theme. He marched towards the door when he stumbled.

Jack pulled his foot away and shot out his arm to steady the man. 'Careful there, mate.' For good measure he gave Forsythe's arm a manly squeeze.

Tommy fell into lockstep with Jack as he left. 'Should we do something?'

Jack shook his head. 'Let the man enjoy himself, while he still can.'

'I see. Everything's under control.'

'It is.' He pulled Tommy to the side.

Mr Whalan and Mr Mackie came down the hallway. 'Good luck, gentlemen,' he said.

They strode on, resplendent in their uniforms and

tapped Mr Forsythe on the shoulder as he made his way towards his cabin. He spun around. For an instant, fear flickered over his face.

'Officers,' he said. 'Is there anything I can do for you?'

'Just a quick word.' Mr Whalan beamed at him. 'The captain would like a chat about certain items.' He held up a metal hook favoured by card sharps. 'This was found in your cabin. We'd also like to see your dice.'

'That's not mine.' Forsythe's eyes bulged.

Jack led Tommy away. 'I told you not to worry.'

Tommy grinned. 'I hope they can throw the book at him.'

'Believe me, they will.'

~

Frances goggled at her plush new surroundings. The suite she found herself in would have been fit for His Majesty himself. Two bedrooms with beds large enough for a family, dressing rooms and a shared bathroom in between took up the back half of the space. In the front, the living room could easily hold an orchestra. Wall-to-wall plush carpet made walking barefoot heaven, although she did not envy the stewards who had to keep it clean.

The colour scheme in gold, turquoise and emerald green emphasised the reddish gold of Evie's hair and her porcelain skin. Frances wondered if the captain had chosen this suite for the simple purpose to make Evie feel like a beautiful princess, after her ordeal.

Or possibly it was the only suite left. One had to be very

rich to afford this luxury. This place humbled Aunt Mildred and Tommy's abode.

What it didn't do was look lived-in. Evie had refrained from setting out a single thing on the gleaming furniture. Her washbag with toiletries hung from a hook in the bathroom, and her few clothes hung in the wardrobe. That was all.

The reading material filled a small inbuilt shelf. Evie hadn't touched it either. A dinner tray with a large metal dome intended to keep meals warm, stood on the coffee table.

'Have you eaten?' Frances asked as she lowered herself onto a pouffe. Evie perched on the edge of a wing chair.

'Not yet,' Evie admitted. 'I'm not that hungry and I was too afraid of spilling something and making a mess. It doesn't feel real.'

'It doesn't,' Frances agreed. She lifted the dome and revealed a fragrant steak pie with potatoes and carrots, and apple custard for dessert. 'But this food is real enough.'

She observed with pleasure that Evie's appetite returned after the first bite. Her friend tucked in until the plate was clean. 'I'm too full for dessert,' she said. 'Do you want it?'

'Save it for later.' Frances bit her lip. 'Did they treat you well in –'

'While I was locked up?' Evie pushed a lock behind her ear. Her fingers trembled a little. 'Yes, they did. Three meals a day, and the chain let me move freely almost to the door.'

'Chains?'

'They could hardly risk me attacking whenever my food was delivered. I don't blame the captain for being cautious.'

Evie hugged herself. 'I don't think a murderer would think twice about hurting someone.'

Frances got goose-bumps. 'I hope they're careful around Mrs Halsall. That woman is evil.'

'If only Larry had never met me, he'd still be alive. Or if he'd been less honourable.'

'I think she would have killed him anyway, if Rosalie had found another admirer, she liked better, or tired of her husband.' Frances swallowed hard. 'Jack said she didn't shed a single tear or ask to see her mother.'

'Maybe it was the shock.' Evie took Frances's hand. Her skin felt icy. 'It is really over, isn't it? This isn't just a dream and I'll wake up and wait for the police to take me away?'

'You're safe,' Frances said. 'Nothing bad can happen to you now.'

'What I don't understand is, why didn't she kill me?'

'There was no guarantee that even then, Larry would have gone through with the marriage. The grieving fiancée has a lot more appeal than the jilted one. And it would have been terribly suspicious if anything had happened to you under the circumstances.' Goosebumps formed on Frances's arms. 'Don't forget, she meant you to be sentenced for murder. Instead, she'll pay for what she has done.'

~

Evie fell into an exhausted sleep. Frances lay next to her in the giant bed. She listened to the regular breathing of her friend. Evie had confessed to having nightmares, so Frances had stayed in her bedroom.

She pulled the blankets up to her chin. Jack thought Evie would not have to give a statement at Mrs Halsall's trial, whenever or wherever that would be. She had been through enough without being reminded that the woman had actively tried to send Evie to the gallows for her own crime.

CHAPTER TWENTY-EIGHT

Breakfast was a hasty affair. Frances had promised to return to Evie as soon as she could, and apart from lunch, she intended to stay in their suite until she had to get ready for her and Uncle Sal's show. They would have their dinner afterwards, as most performers did.

She found Evie poring over a magazine; an old *Tatler* with the society pages from the London scene. There was a photo of Larry, and of Mr Callaghan during a ball. Larry looked carefree and handsome in his tuxedo and dress shirt. Evie ran her fingers over his face on the picture. 'He was the nicest man I've ever met,' she said. 'Do you think I could keep this magazine? Or at least the page?'

'Do you regret saying no?'

Evie smiled under tears. 'Marrying me would have ruined him. Love and romance and all that is all very well, but people would have talked about me and that would have hurt him so. Our worlds don't really mix, do they? At least not in the open and with a wedding band on your finger.'

She reached for a box of tissues and blew her nose. 'We would have had a chance in a place like Australia, but I couldn't ask him to give up his life for me, could I? Except that's what happened anyway.'

'What will you do?'

'The same as always. I'll sing, I'll says, and if I'm lucky it'll pay my bills until I'm too old. Then I'll find something else, maybe as a dresser.' She blew her nose again. 'Let's talk of happier things. What does the tree look like?'

Frances curved a one corner of her mouth. 'It's bonzer. You'll see soon enough for yourself. When you've recovered from the cold that kept you in your bed for a few days.'

Evie's mouth opened.

'That was the original story anyway. We thought it's better than drawing attention to your connection with the case, unless you'd prefer that?'

'Thank you,' Evie said.

'One more night, and you'll be free.'

～

The *Empress of the Sea* arrived in Bombay in the early hours of the morning. Beneath Frances's feet, the ship shuddered as its engines stuttered to stop. Two lascars lowered the gangway, and together with the port officials, two official looking men in civilian clothes came aboard.

Passengers were not allowed outside yet, Frances and Jack had been informed, to make the arrest as discreet as possible. It helped that most of them, like Evie, were still asleep.

Frances pressed her nose against the bullseye in the bedroom of her suite until she saw a quartet of burly sailors with Larry Vaughan's coffin between them solemnly stepping down the gangway.

A tear rolled down her cheek. She silently waved Larry goodbye, as she saw the two official men again. One of them led Mr Forsythe by the elbow. The major's hands were tied at his back and his head drooped.

Frances observed the whole group climb into two a car and drive away into the dawn. Loud noises from the passage told her that people were leaving their cabins. But what had happened to Mrs Halsall? Why didn't the men take her into custody?

CHAPTER TWENTY-NINE

Frances had no opportunity to investigate the puzzle of Mrs Halsall's whereabouts, although that question was uppermost in her mind. Ada and Nancy had been forewarned, and their acting skills helped them hide any surprise as Evie made her appearance together with Frances at the breakfast table.

'What a pleasure to see you out and about again,' Mr Mackie said as he stopped to greet them. He raised his voice in case somebody had managed not to hear him.

Frances stifled a guffaw.

'I hope you're fully recovered from your nasty cold, Miss Miles,' he said.

'I am. Thank you.' Her smile didn't quite have the same luminous quality it used to, but despite the sadness in her eyes she was as lovely as ever.

'Excellent,' Mr Mackie said. 'We've missed you.'

Ada rolled her eyes at his bad acting. Frances mouthed, 'Don't.'

A steward brought their eggs and toast, and Billy tea for Frances, Evie, and for Aunt Mildred at the next table.

'When will we be allowed on shore?' Uncle Sal asked the steward.

'Right after breakfast, sir.'

As soon as Frances had finished her eggs and bacon, she excused herself. Jack did the same, catching up with her outside the doors.

'What happened to you know who?' she asked.

He put a finger on his lips as he led her to her cabin.

Inside, he leant against the closed door. 'There's no need to be afraid,' he said, 'but Mrs Halsall is coming with us to England, to stand trial. The police commissioner has arranged with Captain Grey that she will be kept as a prisoner onboard, with a policeman guarding her. He'll take up his post before we leave port.'

'Does that mean Evie has to appear in court after all?' Frances's nerves jangled. How terrible, after all her friend had been through.

'The confession should be enough, together with witness' statements from the doctor and Mr Whalan. Don't tell Evie that the woman is still travelling with us. Or anyone else, for that matter.'

'Of course not. But won't people ask, if the Halsalls are suddenly no longer to be seen? Or is Rosalie leaving?'

'No.' An amused smile played on Jack's lips. 'The girl has discovered her filial devotion and intends to stick it out with her mum. She even asked permission to visit her. That takes more pluck than I'd credited her with. But enough of that. For us it's over, and we need to get ready for our shore leave.'

Frances stumbled as she stepped off the gangway at Ballard Pier. Uncle Sal had the good sense to spread his legs a little wider until he found his land legs again after their weeks at sea.

She inhaled the pungent air only to cough.

'Wait until we're clear of the ship's funnels,' Jack said. He hailed two taxis. To Frances surprise, he helped her and Aunt Mildred into one, but did not join them.

'Aren't you coming with us?' she asked.

'I'll meet you here in five hours,' he said. 'I don't want you to waste our stay while I have my film rolls developed.'

So much had happened, she'd forgotten all about it.

'If you give me the letter for your family, I'll post it for you.'

She handed him the blue airmail envelope. She'd decided against telling her mother too many things about the journey. That would keep until she came home in a few months. What she had included was the ship's games schedule and a menu, so Mum had enough to entertain the neighbours with. Words like murder and investigation would only scare everyone on her behalf.

Jack closed the door behind Uncle Sal and Tommy. The chauffeur, a slight man with a red turban and an innocent smile, started the engine.

The architecture close to the pier could have been Australian, she thought surprised and a little disappointed. She'd expected something exotic, but although beautiful, the sandstone buildings with their arcades and lion sculptures could have been anywhere.

'It's terribly British, isn't it? The feeling of good old home wherever you go in the Empire where the sun never sets.' Tommy winked at her. 'It gets more exciting, I promise.'

He was right. Ten minutes later, Frances marvelled at cafés with beturbaned waiters, raven-haired women in colourful silk saris, and a camel carrying woven baskets being led into a courtyard.

Tommy bade the chauffeur stop. He handed him a pound note and ordered him to pick them up in good time to return to their ship.

Sweet smells of food, flowers, cardamom and cloves came from everywhere.

'Careful where you step,' Aunt Mildred said as Uncle Sal helped her out of the taxi. 'India has its charms, but cleanliness is not among them.'

True enough, Frances had to sidestep a few animal droppings.

'Tea?' Aunt Mildred steered them towards a café with a tiled interior courtyard. A palm tree in the centre gave off shade for the surrounding tables.

'Memsahib?' A waiter bowed to her before he greeted Frances, Uncle Sal and Tommy.

'We'll have tea and some of your mother's biscuits, Rajeev,' she said.

He bowed again and retreated backwards.

'This is the best café in the neighbourhood,' Aunt Mildred declared with a fond gaze around. 'It hasn't changed since my first visit during the reign of Edward VII. Have you been to India before, Sal?'

'No. Australia and Europe, that's all I've seen in my life.'

'It's a marvellous country,' Tommy said. 'Despite all the British traditions we've enforced upon them, they've kept their soul.'

'I hope you won't say anything of this sort in the Foreign Office.' His aunt frowned at him.

'I'll be the essence of diplomacy.'

'Good. You have to admit, we have brought welcome and much needed progress to this country.'

'Absolutely,' Tommy agreed readily. 'But it always feels like we take more in return than we give to the nations we've added to the empire.' He grinned at her perplexed face. 'Don't be afraid, Aunt Mildred. I can play the fool as easily as the rabble-rouser.'

Aunt Mildred laughed as she slapped his hand.

'What a performer the stage has lost in your nephew,' Uncle Sal said. Frances nodded. Habitually, it was easy to take Tommy as a good-natured, conventional young Englishman with good breeding and a lack of opinions. On the few occasions he allowed them a glimpse behind the façade, he showed a force of character and ideas that reminded her of Jack.

'Are there any nice shops nearby?' she asked. 'I want to buy a Christmas present for Jack.'

'After our tea, I'll take you to an adorable marketplace. It used to be an old caravanserai,' Aunt Mildred promised.

Frances had never seen a more crowded and yet exciting place. British gentlemen and ladies, their servants in tow, haggled in loud voices over prices, while the Indian customers used their hands to do the talking. Glass and brass wares, carvings, and colourful silks jostled for her attention. In one corner, a snake charmer played his flute while the animal swayed to the tune.

Frances took a step back and grasped for Uncle Sal for support.

'The snake is harmless,' Timmy said. 'They're usually defanged. Cruel to the animal, but much safer for everyone.'

Five hours later, they returned to the ship with sore feet and so many parcels, they'd hired a boy to carry them.

Frances had purchased blue and green silk saris, bracelets made of hammered golden disks for her mother and for Jack's, long slippers with upcurled toes for her brother and for Uncle Sal, and a pair of brass bookends in the form of elephants for Jack. Despite all this, she had spent a lot less money than she'd feared.

'Did you have a good day?' Jack carried a bulging parcel and two large manila envelopes as they met at the pier.

'The best,' she said. 'Apart from you not being there.'

'I'm glad to hear that.' He rubbed his scalp, something she'd come to recognise as a sign of distraction.

'Is everything all right?' she asked.

'It's all fine.'

He didn't say any more until they were back on board.

'Take this to my cabin,' he said to Sam, who'd awaited the returning passengers, as he handed him the parcel and one of the envelopes. 'Is the captain in his office?'

Sam's eyes were round as saucers. 'Yes, Sir. Shall I take you to him?'

'No need.' Frances had trouble keeping up with Jack as he set off.

He gave her a reassuring smile. 'It's all good news,

kiddo, so don't worry.' Now her curiosity was seriously piqued.

~

Captain Grey shot him a wary glance as Jack strode in after a short knock. 'Don't tell me you've uncovered another misdeed.'

'Not at all, sir.' Jack threw the envelope on the tables. 'Have a peek inside.'

The captain emptied the envelope. It contained three large photographs. One showed Larry Vaughan dressed up as harlequin, happy and carefree at the bar. The next one pictured Mrs Halsall, sweeping Evie's cigarette case into her evening bag at the costume ball. In the third, her dance partner dipped her, and her fingers reached for the feathers on Evie's dress.

'These photos should be enough to strengthen the case against the lady, should she withdraw her written confession,' Jack said. 'If you could send one of your men to the police station hand them over?'

'What a cold-blooded woman that is.' The captain stared at the damning pictures. 'I'll take care of it straight away.'

'There's no need for that.' Dr Gifford had entered so quietly Jack hadn't heard a thing.

'What are you talking about?' The captain's eyebrows shot up.

'About an hour ago, Mrs Halsall was served tea. She told the man on guard that she needed the stomach powder her doctor had prescribed and that he'd find it in her wash-bag.

Sure enough, there was a box labelled bicarbonate of soda. He gave her the dose she asked for, and then told him she needed to rest.' His mouth set in grim lines. 'And rest she did. The box contained veronal.'

'Suicide?' The doctor locked his hands behind his back. 'Maybe not the worst solution. No trial, and with the confession there's no need for a scandal.'

'How lucky for the daughter,' Jack said.

'Very much so,' the doctor agreed. 'I'd say that's what made that devilish woman do it. She had no escape left, so why drag the daughter down with her?'

'Have you informed Miss Halsall?'

'I thought you'd prefer to take care of it, Captain,' the doctor said. 'If I might suggest informing the consulate and the police as well? And maybe ask if they need to talk to Miss Halsall and would prefer her to take the next ship back home?'

'I'll see to it,' the captain said. 'I can't say I won't be glad to see the last of all of them.'

CHAPTER THIRTY

The rest of the journey passed with pleasing monotony. By the time they'd reached European waters, the other passengers had accepted accidental nicotine poisoning as explanation for Larry Vaughan's death. Dr Gifford had extolled the risks of dropping a cigar butt into one's whisky and fishing it out before finishing one's drink in a lecture as boring as it was long.

Mrs Halsall and Rosalie's departure had been easily explained by their wish to stay with an uncle in India and mourn in privacy.

Only Mr Forsythe's removal was discussed with a degree of honesty and applause for the crew's diligence.

Evie and Nancy spent their free hours teaching Frances a complicated dance routine. Ada acted as choreographer when she wasn't busy giving lessons to her admirer.

Frances had little doubt she wouldn't see the man again once they'd reached London, and Ada said as much herself. Still, she seemed content enough.

'Stop wool-gathering, Frances.' Ada tapped out a

rhythm on the floor. 'You skipped the third beat again.'

Frances wiped her brow. 'Can we slow it down, please?'

'The slower the steps are, the more you're likely to trip up. Positions, girls. From the top.'

The music started again.

~

Two days later, on the final night of the journey, several dreams came true. Evie had her moment of glory with a rendition of "Jingle Bells" and "Zat You, Santa Claus", that earned her a standing ovation.

Frances's hands still smarted from clapping as she tapped and twirled with her new friends through a flawless routine that drew in rousing cheers.

To make these memories last forever, Jack snapped picture after picture from a spot in the wings.

Frances joined him as the girls were finally allowed off-stage for a ten-minute break. Salvatore the Magnificent closed the programme.

Jack massaged her shoulder as she gulped down a glass of water. The waiters served mouth-watering eggnog all around, but that would have to wait.

The drumbeat alerted her. One more minute,

She danced out onto the stage where Salvatore the Magnificent opened his arms as if to embrace his audience.

Their first numbers were taken from their original programme. They had two dozen acts and performed four of them for each show, so the audience wouldn't tire of them. The juggling, knife-throwing and linking rings trick went down without a single hitch.

The throbbing drumbeat started again.

'For the next trick, I'll need help from the audience.' Uncle Sal made a dramatic pause as he scanned the crowd. 'Who is brave enough to risk unleashing magic?'

Tinkerbell yipped. The passengers laughed and clapped.

'A brave little dog, and who will assist him?'

'I will.'

Jack snapped away with his Leica as Aunt Mildred with Tink in her arms swept onto the stage.

Frances took over the little dog, and the drummer beat a staccato as Uncle Sal produced flowers out of Aunt Mildred's dress sleeve. He let her select a card from a deck and made it levitate.

'Is that all you needed me for?' she asked in a carrying tone. The audience laughed.

Uncle Sal took a step back. She shrugged dramatically, reached out behind his ear – and held up a gleaming coin. And another. And another.

With the air of a benevolent fairy godmother she flung them into the audience.

'Got one!' Mr Sanders jumped up and showed off the coin. The audience cheered and whistled as Uncle Sal and Aunt Mildred joined hands and took a bow together.

'Ladies and gentlemen, you were wonderful, as was my new assistant, the magical Lady Mildred, and her furry sidekick, Tinkerbell.'

Tink woofed as he heard his name. Frances let him run to his mistress.

'I've got something to show you,' Jack said to Frances.

Hand in hand, they sauntered to the observation deck.

On one side of the ship, she could see land, dotted with a few lights.

'Look up,' he said.

She craned her neck. Above them, a flurry of snowflakes danced through the air and settled on the glass roof. Frances's heart beat faster with happiness.

The snow still fell as they sailed into the port the next day at noon. The frosty air made her breath plume out, and thousands of chimneys let smoke curl up into the sky.

Frances stood by the rail, arms interlinked with Jack and Uncle Sal, savouring each precious moment. She'd never been this happy before.

'Not a bad sight, is it?' a voice said behind her. Tommy's eyes sparkled as he watched London come closer.

'It's wonderful,' she said. 'And it was bonzer, meeting you and your aunt.'

'Good heavens, child, you sound as if we're parting forever.' Aunt Mildred nudged her nephew aside. 'Sal has already promised me that you and he will help me entertain my guests at one of my parties, and you're more than welcome to stay at my home. I must warn you though that you can't expect much excitement under my roof. But then lightning and murder doesn't strike twice, does it?'

Frances, Jack and Uncle Sal chuckled in unison. 'I guess it doesn't often,' Frances said, her eyes fastened on the city where she'd meet her future in-laws. 'We can do without crime.'

The End

ACKNOWLEDGMENTS

Thank you to all the readers who asked for more adventures with Jack, Frances, and Uncle Sal. You gave me the push to write Murder makes Waves.

A special thanks goes to the members of Facebook group Skye's Mum and Books, who unfailingly offer support, cheer, and adorable pet pictures.

Last, but never least there are my fellow writers Fiona, Linda, Meredith, and Lexie, whose good opinion matters more to me than I can say.

Thank you, every single one, for being there for me on this journey.

If you enjoyed this mystery on the high seas, please consider leaving a review where you bought it or on Goodreads and BookBub. Reviews are important to authors and I want to thank you in advance.

ALSO BY CARMEN RADTKE

Don't miss out on the other Jack and Frances mysteries!

A Matter of Love and Death

Adelaide, 1931. Telephone switchboard operator Frances' life is difficult as sole provider for her mother and adopted uncle. But it's thrown into turmoil when she overhears a suspicious conversation on the phone, planning a murder.

If a life is at risk, she should tell the police; but that would mean breaking her confidentiality clause and would cost her the job. And practical Frances, not prone to flights of fancy, soon begins to doubt the evidence of her own ears - it was a very bad line, after all...

She decides to put it behind her, but it's not easy. Luckily there is the charming, slightly dangerous night club owner Jack. Jack's no angel - six pm prohibition is in force, and what's a nightclub without champagne? But when Frances' earlier fears resurface, she knows that he's the person to confide in.

Frances and Jack's hunt for the truth puts them in grave danger, and soon enough Frances will learn that some things are a matter of love and death ...

Buy it here.

Murder at the Races

Nothing is a dead-cert against a cold blooded killer ...

1931. Frances Palmer is overjoyed when her brother Rob returns to Adelaide as a racecourse veterinarian. But all is not well on the turf, and when a man is murdered, there is only one suspect – Rob.

Frances and her boyfriend, charming night club owner Jack Sullivan, along with ex-vaudevillian Uncle Sal and their friends have only one chance to unmask the real murderer, by infiltrating the racecourse. The odds are against them, but luckily putting on a dazzling show where everything depends on sleight of hand is what they do best.

But with time running out for Rob, the race is on ...

Buy it here.

Meet Jack Sullivan in **False Play at the Christmas Party**, a novelette set in 1928.

A charity ball in aid of veterans sounded like rich pickings ...

Buy it here.

Meet Alyssa Chalmers, Victorian emigrant, reluctant bride, intrepid sleuth.

The Case of the Missing Bride

Setting sail for matrimony – or something sinister?

1862. When a group of young Australian women set sail for

matrimony in Canada, they believe it's the start of a happy new life.

But when one of the intended brides goes missing, only Alyssa Chalmers, the one educated, wealthy woman in the group, is convinced the disappearance is no accident. She sets out to find out what happened.

Has there been a murder?

Alyssa is willing to move heaven and earth to find out the truth. She is about to discover that there is more to her voyage into the unknown than she bargained for, and it may well cost her life ...

Buy it here.

Glittering Death

Gold, wedding bells and murder ...

1862. A group of brides from Australia have arrived in British Columbia, and love is in the air - until the happiness in the prospectors' town "Run's End" is shattered when the hotel-owner is found dead. To make matters worse, something is wrong with the stored gold at the hotel, and an epidemic makes it impossible for anyone to leave town.

The brides pin all their hopes on their friend Alyssa Chalmers to find the murderer and restore peace in their new home. But the killer is cunning, and desperate ...

Buy it here.

Walking in the Shadow

Quail Island, 1909. Jimmy Kokupe is the miracle man.

On a small, wind-blasted island off the east coast of New Zealand a small colony of lepers is isolated but not abandoned, left to live out their days in relative peace thanks to the charity of the townspeople and the compassion of the local doctor and matron of the hospital.

Jimmy Kokupe is a miracle: he's been cured. But he still carries the stigma, which makes life back on the mainland dangerous and lonely. To find a refuge, he's returned to the camp to care for his friend, fellow patient old Will, and disturbed young Charley.

Healed of his physical ailments and dreaming of the girl he once planned to follow to a new life in Australia, Jimmy meets 'the lady', the island caretaker's beautiful but troubled wife who brings their food. Can she help Jimmy forget his difficult past and overcome his own prejudices towards his mixed parentage, and find the courage to risk living in freedom?

Buy it here.

You can catch up with Carmen Radtke on her website (www.carmenradtke.com), on twitter or on Goodreads or follow her on Bookbub.